About the Book

One moment nineteen-year-old Roley Rolandson was happily delivering Christmas packages along his mail route—the next, he was in the hospital virtually helpless and unable to see. All Roley could remember was a dog hitting him from behind, a blinding flash, then nothing. . . .

Faced with permanent blindness, Roley rejects everything and everyone who might help him—until two young friends, Susan and Steven, do break through some of Roley's resentment and persuade him to apply for a guide dog.

Roley enters a Training Center where he is given Mick, a golden Labrador retriever, the pick of the lot. But the struggle has only begun. For Roley rejects Mick from the beginning even though she constantly tries to win his respect and affection.

Dorothy Clewes tells the dramatic story of a boy's struggle to come to terms with life and to face the future with determined hope. The story is tense and moving, told with real insight into a tragic human problem lived out with courage.

GUIDE DOG

BY

Dorothy Clewes

ILLUSTRATED BY

Peter Burchard

*"One thing I know, that, whereas I was
blind, now I see."*
St. John, Chapter 25

Coward-McCann   New York

Acknowledgments

My grateful thanks are due to Mr. George Werntz, Jr., Vice-President and Secretary of The Seeing Eye, Morristown, New Jersey, U.S.A., for time and trouble extended to me at his Center for dog guides; also to Mr. R. D. Cuddy, Public Relations Officer to Guide Dogs for the Blind in England for his help in arranging for me to visit the Training Centers at Bolton and again at Exeter to cover all stages in the Course of Dogs and Blind Students.

I am also deeply indebted to Mr. D. G. Carver, Controller at Bolton and to Mr. J. P. Weeks, Controller at Exeter for the valuable time they gave me explaining and demonstrating the technical details of their work in its different stages. I would also like to recognize here the help and inspiration given me— wittingly and unwittingly—by so many blind persons themselves. I hope that some of my admiration for the movement, the students and the dogs shows through this story.

Any errors of fact are, of course, my own.

Contents

For Richard Hough
in admiration

1   *Mail Early for Christmas*

At 6:30 on a morning before Christmas the alarm on Roley Rolandson's bedside table rang shrilly. He put out a searching hand and switched it off. For a moment it looked as if he was going to turn over and go to sleep again—and then he stretched himself hugely, threw back the bedclothes and tumbled out.

At 6:45, after a not-too-wet wash in the bathroom, he was dressed and down in the dining room eating the breakfast his mother had left for him the night before—coffee from a flask, a thick bacon sandwich, an apple. Under the apple there was a note from his mother: DON'T GO OUT WITHOUT YOUR SCARF. The scarf was there under the note and was folded on the top of a pile of books. The note went on to say: THE DOCTOR LEFT THESE FOR YOU LAST NIGHT. DON'T LOOK AT THEM NOW OR YOU'LL BE LATE. *Medicine as a Career, Gray's Anatomy, Biology,* Roley read from the printing on the spines and put them down reluctantly. They'd have to wait until this evening. He dutifully wrapped the scarf around his neck, struggled into his coat with its official armband, pulled on wool gloves, and went out into the still dark, frosty morning.

The streets were deserted and his footsteps rang loudly on the hard pavement. A few lights shone from behind curtained windows but for the most part the houses were black etchings on a gray canvas. The air struck crisp and clean. It might snow before the day was through, the smell of it was there.

At 7:45, Roley walked into the Post Office, through a swing door and into a bright cavern of light and noise: counters piled high with parcels; sacks open-necked and overflowing with letters and packages. The extras, boys like himself, were already collecting their bags, contents sorted for their allotted areas by the night men. There was the usual good-natured banter and leg-pulling—

"Make way for the workers."

"The first ten years are the worst, boy."

"Hope you had your sunshine breakfast this morning: you'll need it."

Roley found his own bag and lifted it to slip the broad webbing halter over his head. The bag was heavier than it had been yesterday. That would be because of last night's television appeal: "Positively the last day for certain delivery for Christmas," the announcer had cheerfully threatened. There must have been a real stampede to the letter boxes to produce this much, Roley thought.

At 8, he humped his way out of the Post Office and into the bitter cold of the street. He wasn't grumbling. He'd taken on the job because he'd wanted to. He'd done the same thing the last three Christmases ever since he'd become sixteen, which was the earliest age the Post Office would hire extras. The deep dark had given place now to steel gray and actually a powdering of snow was drifting about in a halfhearted way, as if it was really too cold to do much about it. It might be a white Christmas after all, and that would make it Roley's first. It would be great to see it like that, the way it looked on fifty percent of the Christmas cards in his bag. If it tried really hard there might be tobogganing on the heath—it was hilly enough there to make it worthwhile, and the pond might freeze hard enough for skating.

"Hey—you're doing Park Road, aren't you?"

Roley swung around and waited for the owner of the voice to catch up with him. He knew him by sight, saw him sometimes in his own part of town—a boy a bit younger than himself, couldn't be much over seventeen but he'd shot up since he'd seen him last: a six-footer now or not far off, and big with it. The boy was holding out a parcel sealed with red wax: important-looking. "Actually it's for Park Place, but you're nearer there than I'll be. It's a return."

Roley took the parcel from him and screwed up his eyes to read the writing on the label—typewriting on a faint ribbon and not very good typing at that. THE MINISTER FOR INVENTIONS, WHITEHALL, LONDON, W. 1. it read and across it was stamped: *Return to Sender*.

"What's wrong with it?" Roley asked him. "It looks all right to me."

"No such Ministry. You'd expect a professor to know better, wouldn't you?" He pointed at the sender's name and address on the side of the parcel: *Prof. W. O. Flint, The Gables, Park Place*. "Or maybe not: professors are supposed to be absentminded. He's lucky to get it back."

"As a matter of fact I've always wondered about that house," Roley said. It stood back from the road behind a high brick wall and its twin gables and the chimneys were all you could see of it. He hadn't known who lived there. "I expect it's something he's invented," he said, slipping the parcel into his bag. "I'd like to know what."

"It's a legal offense to open a post office package," the boy said. "I know because I've read up on it. I'm going in for Law—starting college after Christmas. What are you going to do?"

"Medicine," Roley told him. He'd wanted to be a doctor for as long as he could remember. Lately people had started saying he had the right kind of hands, whatever that meant. More important at the moment, he thought, was having the right kind of brain. "I don't know if I'll manage to pass the exams," he said. "They're tough—but it's what I want to do more than anything else." He'd passed his G.C.E. and A levels: now he was waiting to hear from the university.

"That's a real job, that is," the boy said, admiringly. "It's a long training though, isn't it? Expensive, too."

"Yes—and my people aren't all that well off," Roley said. "That's why I do this and anything else I can get hold of. Law sounds interesting, too."

"I guess I feel the same way about it as you feel about medicine," the boy answered. He said in a moment: "I've seen you around, haven't I?"

"Yes. I've seen you, too. I'm Roley. Roley Rolandson. We live in Heath View."

"We live in Oakwood Drive. My name's Steven. Steven Lawrance." He added: "Are you any relation of Harold Rolandson, the Italian tutor at the technical college?"

"He's my father," Roley told him.

"I go to a class there once a week," Steven said. "My Italian wasn't bad at school and I want to keep it up. Next year with any luck I'll go and practice on the natives."

"Gosh—I'd like to travel around. Be years before I can, though." Roley often thought about it, seeing new places, old places. His father had lived in Italy as a boy and talked a lot about it, but a schoolmaster's salary didn't run to luxuries like travel—not for three, anyway, and as far afield as Italy.

"It'll still be there when you can go," Steven said. "Places keep on getting easier to get to, as well."

A milk truck rattled by; a few muffled figures stood at bus stops, stamping their feet. The streets were waking up.

"This is where we part company," Steven said.

They'd come to where the road forked, running
away to the right and to the left.

"Be seeing you," Roley said.

"Not for a bit, you won't," Steven said. "This is my
last round. This afternoon we go to Cornwall for
Christmas."

"*Arrivederci*, then," Roley called after him.

At 8:15, Roley crossed the street into Park Road.
It was a pleasant road, tree-lined, iron-gated, with rail-
ings enclosing tiny gardens, and straight paths leading
up to the front doors. What Roley liked about the job
was that although most of the houses were as alike as
if they'd been run off a conveyer belt, inside they were
all different: one would be bursting with activity when
the door opened to his ring, everyone in a frenzy, up
late as usual, not time to sit down properly for breakfast. Others oozed heavy respectability, no rush to
answer the door, organized calm reigning supreme.
Some still showing blank curtained windows, two rings
on the bell before a tousled, dressing-gowned figure
drew back the bolts. He took the first bundle from his
sack—three cards and a letter for No. 1—and pushed
on the bell.

In a way it was like playing at Santa Claus, Roley
thought as he made his way down the road, handing
over intriguing-looking packages, fat squashy envel-
opes—and people dressed up packages nowadays with
colored seals and fancy papers so that they really looked
ready for the Christmas tree. And Christmas trees
themselves blossomed in some of the windows,
branches sprouting candles like flowers, tinsel spark-
ling, and some of the doors opened onto halls festooned

with paper chains and balloons and holly and mistle-
toe. He wasn't so old it didn't whet his appetite for his
own Christmas. Two loads of aunts and uncles and five
cousins were coming to stay; the place would be bursting at the seams but it was something that happened
every year and wouldn't be Christmas without their all
being together. When it was over, Roley's father always
said "Never again"—but was first with plans when
next year came around. They had seats for the panto-
mime the day after Christmas. They'd just about take
a whole row. It was going to be great.

At 8:30, Roley handed over the last of the letters
and packages. His bag was empty now except for the
parcel to be returned to The Gables, Park Place. It was
only a five-minute walk away: actually he could get
back to the Post Office that way without retracing his
footsteps. He crossed the road and turned up the drive
which led into Park Place. In the summer he was here
most evenings, playing on the tennis courts. They
were good courts, hard and fast, and in the club where
Roley was a member he was one of their crack players.
Now, leaf-strewn and with the gardens and shrubberies
behind them stripped bare, it was hard to imagine that
only a few short weeks ago he'd been sweating it out
there in shorts and open-necked shirt. He was still
thinking about the tennis he'd played and how he'd do
better next season when he found himself in front of
The Gables. He took the parcel out of his bag. It was
pretty heavy for so small a package. He wondered again
what it might be. Maybe a kitchen gadget—the kind
his mother was always buying but which usually ended
up stuffed away at the back of a drawer. Or a television

gadget would be a good idea—something that would switch off the awful commercials which came on the moment you'd start to get interested in the play.

At 8:45 exactly, he lifted the heavy handle of the black oak, iron-studded door and stepped into a court-yard.

The dog must have been behind the door. Roley didn't see him. He was only aware of a shadow bound-ing up from behind simultaneously with excited bark-ing. The heavy body caught him on the elbow and the package he had been holding leapt out of his hand. It rose a couple of inches and then fell at his feet. He bent down to pick it up. There was a sharp explosion, a blinding flash, and then—nothing.

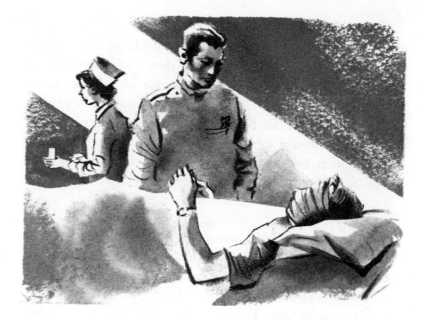

2   *Suspense*

It was odd, Roley thought, that the room was so dark. Dark and yet full of sounds. Strange sounds; a blur of voices he didn't recognize, the light clatter of metal on china, the ring of footsteps on a wooden floor. He closed his eyes and tried to reassemble his thoughts. That was another strange thing, the way his mind would not seem to come up with a clear, straight answer to his thoughts. It was as if it was working in a fog of slow motion. His limbs felt the same way— heavy and uncoordinated. He felt tired, too. Well, maybe not tired but drowsy. Unreal. But he wasn't dreaming, he was sure of that. He lay still, gathering strength to start the process of thinking all over again. If he could hear people moving about why couldn't he see them? This time, like the brush of a finger on a sensitive nerve, his mind answered, and in reply he lifted a hand to his face—and at once, as if the movement had been a signal, a voice spoke:

"Well, hello there. How are you feeling now?" It was a young voice, bright and cheerful—or was it perhaps a shade too cheerful?

Roley's hand, exploring, came to rest on a soft swathe of material. A bandage.

The voice spoke again, this time nearer, and at the same moment a hand closed over his and gently drew it from his face.

"Stay quiet and I'll get Sister. She said to tell her the moment you woke."

"Sister? What is this? Where am I?" He knew before she answered him, thoughts tugging free now from the cotton-wool morass that had been smothering them. There had been a door—opening onto a courtyard. He'd been delivering a parcel. That was it: the Christmas delivery. He could feel the package again in his hand, heavier than it should have been for its size— and then something had sprung him from behind. A dog—

"You were in an accident," the voice told him, crisp now and matter-of-fact, and said again, placing his exploring hand under the bedclothes and tucking the sheets firmly across his chest: "Stay quiet and I'll get Sister."

He felt no compulsion to move this time. He lay back on the pillow and let the thoughts flow free.

There had been an explosion—and then nothing. He'd been cut about the face, that was the reason for the bandages. He tried, very cautiously, moving the muscles of his face. There was no answering pain. Perhaps around the cheekbones a slight stiffness— nothing more. He relaxed. For a moment he had had a vision of a smashed and broken face, but everything seemed to be working: his mouth, his nose twitching rabbit-wise under the bandage, his eyelids. He blinked behind the all-embracing cloth and the lids responded. He had a headache, though, a mother-and-father of one. He could feel the dull throb gathering strength as if the throwing off of so many thoughts had given it a freedom of its own. It swelled and receded in an even, gentle rhythm, absorbing all sound so that the man's voice penetrated Roley's mind as from a great distance.

"Draw the curtains, Sister, and I'll take a look at him while I'm here."

"I wasn't going to disturb you, Doctor, but the parents keep telephoning."

The metallic rattle of rings on a pole, the soft movement of air on his face, pulled Roley back from his deep concentration of pain. He moved his head in the direction of the new voices. There was a note of deference in the woman's voice but an authority, too, that the bright, cheerful one had lacked.

"I'll speak to them myself when I've got the full picture," the man's voice said. His hand touched Roley's shoulder. "Now, young man. I'm Doctor Benson. You came in this morning. Can you remember anything of what happened?"

Two pairs of hands were helping him into a sitting position in the bed, the young nurse was back again, her touch lighter than the Sister's. She wasn't as expert at this job and he tried to put in a bit of effort of his own.

"I was delivering a parcel—and it exploded. I don't remember anything more until I woke up a few moments ago."

The nurse was unwinding the bandage; her hands as they passed around his head smelled faintly of carbolic.

"That was nine hours ago," Doctor Benson told him. "You've had a good sleep. How do you feel?"

"I've got a raging headache," Roley said. "Otherwise I suppose I don't feel too bad. What was it—in the parcel?"

"A firecracker," the doctor said. "Someone's idea of a joke."

There was something in the way he said it that struck fear in Roley's heart. He said, quickly, "It hasn't done too much damage, has it? I mean—it doesn't hurt me anywhere—except for the headache."

"You caught it full in the face. You've got a burn or two on the cheekbone but that will soon heal—and your eyelashes will grow again."

The nurse was coming to the end of the unbandaging, he could feel the pressure of it lessening—but no light filtered through.

"How's that?" the doctor asked him. "You've drops in your eyes, of course—but how much can you see?"

The bandage was off. His eyes were open. He blinked his lids, moving his head this way and that in

growing panic. "Nothing. I can't see a thing. I can't see—"

"Now take it easy, take it easy." Doctor Benson's steadying voice checked his threshing questions, a firm hand on his arm. "Don't let's jump to wild conclusions. I haven't examined you yet—and I'm not an eye surgeon. We can pull plenty of those characters out of the bag when we're ready. Lift your head for me and let me take a look."

It seemed forever before the doctor finished his examination. The silence in the little cubicle had reached a point for Roley that was almost unbearable when Doctor Benson said, "We'll let Sir William Clarke have a look at you. What he doesn't know about eyes isn't worth knowing."

"You mean—you can't do anything?" In Roley's ears his voice sounded unreal.

"It isn't my job to do anything but get you on your feet again, and that isn't going to be any problem. What I can tell you is that your eyes are healthy."

"They're healthy but I can't see. That's fine," Roley said, bitterly.

"You can't see at the moment: well, that's understandable. You've suffered a tremendous shock and shock can blind—temporarily. Before we do anything else we've got to get you back to normal. Right now the most important thing for you is rest and that's something I can make sure you do get." Roley felt his arm lifted and a brief dabbing on his forearm of what felt like damp cotton wool. "You'll feel only the smallest prick . . ."

3   *Nurse Lambert Talks*

It was dark when next Roley woke, a strange darkness unrelieved by any shadowy light—and then memory came flooding back explaining the bed that was narrower than his own and harder and with more pillows than he was used to. He was in the hospital. He hadn't been able to see and they'd bandaged his face again. He lifted a hand—but there was no bandage there. Shock could blind, the doctor had said—temporarily. He tried not to panic, but he'd slept since then, deeply and dreamlessly, and there was no difference, no difference.

20

A voice, a man's voice said, "I was thinking it was about time you woke up. I'm Police Constable Sutton."

Roley turned in the direction of the new voice. "Police Constable?"

"I've been detailed to make inquiries about . . . the accident. . . ." The constable's voice faltered.

"Oh." Roley made an effort to clear his mind, to think back.

"I don't want to worry you," Constable Sutton said, "but if you did feel like giving me a statement—"

"He'll have his breakfast first, Constable. If you'd like to help him with it you'd be making yourself useful." It was the young voice, very bright and very cheerful. "I didn't wake you before, you were having such a lovely sleep," she said to Roley. "Can you sit up now? You'll feel better after a nice cup of tea."

They were behaving as if nothing had happened to him. "I'm blind," he shouted. "I'm still blind."

"I know," the nurse said, "but it's early days yet. Sir William Clarke's coming in to see you this afternoon. He's a wonderful man. He'll know what's best to do. Come on, now. I've poured your tea out." She guided his hand to a table in front of him and closed his hand around the cup. "There's buttered toast there, too," guiding his other hand to the plate. "Now you're not to worry him until he's finished every crumb," she told the constable.

The tea was good, hot and sweet and strong. They gave you sweet tea for shock, Roley remembered, but he liked it that way anyway. In a moment he fumbled with his other hand in search of the toast and was grateful to the constable for not rushing in to find it for him. Tea and toast was easy. He said quickly, before his mind could pursue other less simple tasks, "What time is it?"

"Half past eight," the constable said, and added, "in the morning."

"When did it happen?" Roley couldn't bear to speak the actual words.

"Yesterday morning—about this time, I understand. "You've slept the clock around."

"It hasn't done me any good, though. I'm blind. They're all pretending it's going to be all right, aren't they? Well—you heard them. What do they say when I'm out of earshot?"

"I wouldn't know," the constable said. "They don't talk to me. I've been sitting here waiting for you to wake up so I could get a statement from you."

"There isn't anything to tell. I was delivering a parcel, a dog jumped me and it fell and exploded. I don't remember anything more until I woke up here."

"Tell me about the parcel. How big was it?"

"Oh . . . three or four inches by about two, and perhaps a couple of inches deep. It was heavy, I remember that. And I remember wondering what it was because it had been returned from the Minister of Inventions—and that's why it was returned, because there isn't any such ministry. You'd expect a professor to know better, wouldn't you?" The last words had a familiar ring as if he'd spoken them before or heard them spoken, but his brain wouldn't work it out for him. "I was delivering it to The Gables, Park Place. Professor W. O. Flint." He remembered that plainly enough. "You might get to know more if you questioned him."

"We have," the constable said.

"So what has he got to say for himself? It's a punishable offense to send explosive material through the mails, even I know that. I hope he knows he's got something coming to him."

"He didn't send it—or that's what he's saying."

"Can he prove he didn't?" The professor needn't think he was going to get out of it as easily as that. The man had a summons coming to him. If he thought he was going to get off scot-free, he could think again.

"He's working on it," the constable said.

"Well, I've told you all I know," Roley said, and added: "Have you ever heard of Sir William Clarke?"

"Another inventor?" the constable asked.

Roley shook his head. "Forget it." Constable Sutton could only think of his job. Well, that was understandable. The only thing he, Roley, could think of was his eyes. "He's an eye specialist" Roley told him. "They're getting him in to see me. He'd better come up with the answer, that's all." And if there wasn't an answer? Roley didn't dare explore that avenue of thought. He said, quickly, "I can't help you, and right now I can't think of anything else but whether I'm going to see again."

"Of course," Constable Sutton said. "I understand. And you have helped me quite a lot."

Roley could sense the policeman's discomfort, his awkwardness. Any moment now he was going to say he was sorry and of course it would be all right.

"Don't worry, boy. It'll be all right, you'll see. They

can do pretty well anything nowadays. You'll be up and about and seeing more than you ought to before you can say Boo. You mark my words."

There it was, the kindly pressure of a hand on his shoulder indicating sympathy. He's nice, he means well, Roley tried to tell himself, but he doesn't believe one sweet word he's saying. He made an effort: "I'd like to know—if you find out anything."

"Sure, sure." The reassuring pat again, and then on a brisk note of relief: "I have to get back now, but I'll be in to see you."

After he'd gone, Roley slept again and then the bright little nurse fed him his lunch—or as much of it as he could swallow. Not being able to see stripped you of so much more than sight. Sir William Clarke had better come up with an answer.

"What else are you called besides Nurse?" he asked. If you talked you couldn't think.

"Lambert."

He liked the crisp, businesslike voice. All the same she didn't sound more than about seventeen.

"I meant, what goes in front of Lambert?"

"Nurse," she said.

"Is that part of the training?" he asked her.

"What?"

"Not getting too friendly with the patient?"

"That's right," she said.

"Doesn't it make any difference that I'm going to be a doctor?"

He thought the little sound she made was a sharp intake of her breath, but if it was she covered it up immediately with "You should know better than to ask, then, shouldn't you?"

A voice spoke—the older voice: "Mr. Rolandson's parents are here," and to Roley: "It isn't visiting time but we're making an exception."

It's what he had longed for—and dreaded: to see his mother and father. Only he wasn't going to be able to see them and the dread was that his mother would break down. It wasn't beyond the bounds of possibility that he would, too. He took a deep breath.

"Darling—" There was the smallest break in his mother's voice but she mastered it immediately.

His father hid his feelings behind the bluff and hearty greeting he kept for difficult occasions. "Well, son—you got yourself into a hospital sooner than you expected."

It was easier to talk, then. "I feel fine, Mom, really I do. Sir William Clarke's seeing me this afternoon. He knows all there is to know about eyes. Shock can cause temporary blindness. That's what the doctor here said, Dad—but Sir William Clarke is the eye king, they all say that. He'll know."

Silence suddenly filled the little cubicle and then they were all talking at once.

"Of course, darling. He's a wonderful man. Matron has been telling us—"

"It's going to be all right, son, you'll see. Sir William Clarke's the top: they don't come any higher than he."

"But—supposing he can't do anything?" The words, until this moment, had been only a nagging, unacknowledged thought at the back of Roley's mind. Now he couldn't hold them back any longer.

"Don't cross your bridges until you get to them."
His father's voice was sharp as if the fear was there in
his own mind, too—a fear that he wasn't prepared to
acknowledge.

"The doctor says you can come home at the end of
the week, unless . . . of course . . . Sir William . . ."
His mother's words trailed away.

"That'll be great. Great." What did you do when
you got home if you couldn't see? What did you do
anywhere? Nothing, that was the answer to that one.
Nothing, nothing, and forever nothing. He said
quickly, because it wasn't going to be like that, it
couldn't be, "Those books the Doc left for me, I can't
wait to get into them. As soon as this . . . blackout's
lifted."

"Dr. Graham's coming in to see you tonight after
his surgery," his father said. "You're out of his hands
in here but he's going to have a word with Sir William
Clarke after—"

The Sister's voice broke in. "I'm afraid I have to ask
you to go now. You can come in again this evening.
Visiting hours are from seven-thirty to nine o'clock—
and by that time Sir William will have seen him."

"That's right, Mom. It isn't anything really. Well,
it hasn't spoilt my beauty. The scar won't show at all
in a bit. Nurse said so." He was suddenly a small boy
again apologizing for the black eye and bleeding nose
honorably won in battle with the boy next door—only
this wasn't a black eye and a bleeding nose. "It isn't
anything," he said again, "really it isn't." He could
feel her crying although she wasn't making a sound and
he couldn't bear it. "It'll be all right, really it will."

It was a relief when they'd gone, but it was frightening, too—as if suddenly he'd been cut off from them, from everyone. Now he was on his own. Why didn't Sir William come if he was coming? But what if he couldn't do anything, either?

Nurse Lambert's voice said, "I like your people, they're sweeties. You're lucky, you know. I lost mine."

"You mean—they're dead?" For a moment his fearful thoughts for himself receded to make way for her awful pronouncement. "Both of them?"

"Yes—in a car accident. That was the only good thing about it, that they died together."

It was happening every day but somehow when you knew the someone it had happened to it was worse, much worse. "How long ago?" he asked her.

"Last year. A lunatic in a sports car tried to overtake them on a wet road and just couldn't make it. He pulled in to avoid a truck coming in the opposite direction and the three crashed together. The truck driver was the only one who escaped."

"You poor kid." Odd how you couldn't tell about people. She'd sounded as if she hadn't a care in the world. Roley said, "Have you brothers and sisters?"

"No, I'm an only child."

"What did you do?"

"Went on living here. It's funny, your world comes to an end but suddenly you're into the next day and then the next. And it's easier to carry on than to sit down and think about what's happened to you. I didn't know what else to do, anyway."

"What do you do for holidays?" Home was a place that was always there.

"Oh, I have uncles and aunts. They make a fuss over me."

"And so they should." He'd suddenly been prepared to be furious if they hadn't.

"I couldn't have been easy to live with but I've stopped being sorry for myself now, and I've stopped being sorry for Mum and Dad because at least they went together and that's how they would have wanted it."

Talking with her, Roley had, for a moment, forgotten about himself. But now voices, matron's and a man's deep voice brought his thoughts rushing back.

"Now Mr. Rolandson, here is Sir William—"

4   *Sir William Pronounces*

It couldn't be true. In a moment he'd wake up and know it was all a ghastly nightmare, but Sir William's words were still ringing in Roley's ears, the words that mattered: "the optic nerve destroyed . . . . nothing that surgery could do."

There'd been a lot more that Roley had only half listened to about it being a tragedy that this should happen to anyone so young, that he'd find other senses compensating, becoming sharper, more aware. He must be thankful that there was no disfigurement and that nowadays there was a very real place in the world for a blind person. He'd asked Roley what he'd been going to do and when Roley told him, he'd done his best to see comfort in that, too: some of the best physiotherapists were blind, this was something they could do almost better than their sighted colleagues. Roley could still study—in Braille—and attend college. He must see his future now as a new way of life.

A new way of life! It was the end of living as far as he was concerned and it was no use anybody trying to gloss it over. They were his eyes that weren't going to see again. From now on he was going to be dependent on someone else seeing for him, fetching and carrying for him, taking him out for an airing as if he were a child again: less than a child again, much, much less. It didn't bear thinking about—and yet he couldn't focus his mind on anything else.

Suddenly at his shoulder Nurse Lambert said, "Here's your tea. I brought it before but Sir William was here."

Roley pushed against the table trolley. "I don't want it. I don't want anything."

"I know you don't but I'll get into trouble if I take it back."

He allowed her to put his fingers around the cup and obediently lifted it to his lips, drained it and put it down. He said, "He can't do anything. You know, don't you? I'm blind. I'm never going to see again."

"Yes, I know—but you're alive and you've got your family, and you have a job you want to do and you're going to be able to do it."

"Are you counting my blessings for me?" He couldn't keep the bitterness out of his voice.

"Yes. I'm trying to save you banging your head against a brick wall. What's done's done. There's nothing you can do about it. You're only going to hurt yourself by not facing up to it."

"In case you thought I was, I'm not that kind of a noble character, the one with the stiff upper lip. All I can think of right now is that I'm never going to see again, that I'm going to be dependent on someone else for the rest of my life, that I'm going to be a kind of— second- or third-class citizen allowed to do some fumbling job out of pity and charity."

"I wonder why you wanted to be a doctor," Nurse Lambert said, "when you've such a low opinion of the medical profession. Being blind doesn't exempt you from exams, you know. You pass or fail like everyone else—on your own merit. You'd better take a look at that, too."

"Physiotherapy, that's all that's left for me. Pummel- ing a lot of old so-and-so's who've let themselves run to seed. Well, you can keep it."

"You don't know much about it, do you, or you wouldn't be so scornful. A doctor or a surgeon can give everything he's got but it isn't going to do a patient any good if that last final touch isn't taken care of. It's—it's like wrapping up a package and then not bothering to tie it so that all the work that's gone before comes undone. Medicine's teamwork, but ob- viously all you were out for was the glory all to your- self."

All she was saying was true, he knew that with one part of him but the other part was uppermost and wouldn't admit it. "You can keep it," he said again.

"I'd have made a lousy doctor, anyway; you're right about that."

"It's too early to know what you're going to do," she said, her voice soft in a first show of sympathy. "It's too early to talk about it. Getting through today will be the worst thing you've got to do—and the next day and the next. After that you'll go on living, like I have, because there's nothing else you can do."

There *were* other things you could do, Roley thought. Like taking a running jump away from it, or doping yourself up so that you didn't have to think about it anymore—but she would never have had thoughts like that.

She pushed something else into his hand, a small glass. "It's a sedative," she told him. "You've still a lot of resting to do. It'll be time enough then to make decisions."

Voices woke him, Matron's and another that he knew: Doctor Graham's. He stirred himself and the doctor said, "Well, a fine postman you turned out to be."

The known and friendly voice broke him. Surprisingly, eyes could weep even though they couldn't see. He said, taking the handkerchief the doctor offered him, "I'm sorry. I—I didn't know I was going to do that."

The doctor's hand pressed Roley's knee understandingly. "D'you know something? It's what I'd prescribe—often—if I could. Nothing to be ashamed of, letting yourself go. Do you good. Now," he said, taking back the sodden handkerchief, "we've got to look at this sensibly and constructively. The damage is done so it's no use belly-aching about it. Right?"

Roley nodded because he couldn't trust his voice. Everything everybody was saying was right, he knew that, but when you were at the receiving end it wasn't so easy as that to take.

"We'll get you back home and by that time I'll have been in touch with the Association for the Blind. We'll have you learning Braille and when you've mastered that we'll get you into college and you can go ahead with your studies."

"I'm scrubbing that out," Roley said.

"You mean—you're throwing up the idea of medicine?"

"Well, let's face that, too. It was a real doctor I wanted to be."

"Look, my dear boy, all physiotherapists aren't blind, some doctors actually choose that as their profession rather than anything else. It's just that a blind person is mostly better at it than a sighted one. And don't make any mistake about it, it's a good living. You'll probably make much more at that than being a poor old G.P. like me."

"But you chose to be a G.P."

"Well, we're facing up to the fact that you haven't the same choice, aren't we?" Doctor Graham reminded him. "You know, I'm not going to be able to help you if I don't give it to you straight, and you wouldn't want me not to. That's something you'll appreciate when you have your own practice. We don't like telling people straight. It's much easier and pleasanter to jolly them along, but it's our job. And something else: maybe there's a reason for what's happened. Perhaps you're meant to do this rather than anything else."

"Oh—religion," Roley said scornfully. "Divine guidance."

"That's right. We're pretty smart with our trips into outer space and plans for life on the moon or some other planet, but we don't know all the answers on this one by a long shot. I'm not so cocksure of myself that I think I know what it's all about."

"If there is any divine guidance," Roley said, "I'd like to see it directed into-leading someone to catch the character who mailed that parcel."

"Well, at least we can promise you that," Doctor Graham said. "I'm one of those people who believe that justice catches up with you sooner or later."

"You just believe," Roley said. "It's funny, I thought I did until this happened but nothing makes sense anymore."

"Give yourself time," the doctor said, "it will." He got up from his perch on the bed. "I hope you're not going to dislike me for this, but I've told your people not to come in again tonight. You've all had as much as you can take for one day."

Relief surged through Roley. He'd been thinking all the time about his parents' next visit, wanting them to come and yet dreading their coming, dreading the effort he was going to have to make to sound cheerful, to keep from breaking up as he had done in front of Doc Graham. He'd got through today, almost. Tomorrow it would be easier. At least that was Nurse Lambert's theory.

"And I'll be home by the end of the week?"

"I'll take you myself," the doctor promised him.

5   *A Voice Out of the Blue*

"The new term starts next week," Doctor Graham said. "You live in—and you'll learn a lot more than Braille. You'll learn how the others cope, swap experiences. You'll lose the feeling that you're the only one this has happened to, make some good friends."

"And how long does it take—to learn Braille?"

Even for Doctor Graham Roley couldn't work up any enthusiasm over the other tidbits he was throwing down; all he was interested in was getting on with the job of learning to read—all over again. Without that he was just a pair of ears, listening: to people talking with a desperate brightness to entertain him; to the radio, which at least didn't demand anything from you in return.

"Three months average—but of course it'll take time before you can read easily and without effort," Doctor Graham told him. "From there you can go on to your physiotherapy course."

"I told you, I'm not interested."

"You'll change your mind," Doctor Graham told him confidently. "And I promise not to say I told you so."

"He knows you better than you know yourself," his mother said when the doctor had gone, "and so he should, he's known you all your life." Doctor Graham had become a good friend as well as their doctor from the time they had first come to live in Barnwood, before Roley had been thought of. What they would have done without his help and support in these last days she couldn't imagine. After the first shock there had been the acceptance of all Roley's blindness was going to mean, and now the fear that this cruel blow might change a happy, bright and eager boy into a sour and bitter young man.

"He's doing his stuff," Roley said. "Jollying the patient along until he gets used to the idea."

"He's a wise man and you'll do well to listen to him," his mother said.

"I am listening," Roley said. "It's all I can do. I'm getting better at it all the time."

"Oh, darling—"

"I'm sorry, Mother." He hated himself for the sharp retort that was always there, but it was out before he could stop it. "I can't help it. I haven't got used to the idea yet, that's all."

"I know, darling. We're all trying to make it easier for you but we aren't used to it yet either."

"Don't try so hard then, *please*. Apart from—what's happened—I'm not any different. I'm still me. I don't want any special treatment."

It was almost worse now that he was home—all attention concentrated on him, the house made to revolve around him, the feeling he was being watched all the time. Actually he could find his way around the house now, up and down the stairs to his own room— just so long as no one moved anything.

At the end of his first week at home he'd had a visitor.

"Well, aren't you going to say you're pleased I've come?"

The voice sent him spinning back to those first few days. "Nurse Lambert."

"I'm Susan off duty—to my friends," she said.

"It was nice of you to come," Roley said. In his own home he felt self-conscious, shy of letting her see how delighted he was that she hadn't forgotten him. Automatically he got to his feet to give her his chair. She accepted it unhesitatingly and made no attempt to guide him to the one on the other side of the fireplace.

When he was settled she said, "You look fine. Tell me, how is it going?"

"I go to school—to learn Braille—next week," he told her. "It's up in town and I live in."

"I'll come to see you on my day off," Susan promised.

"I'd like that," he said, and added defensively, "but you don't have to, you know."

"I know I don't, I'd just like to. I know where the school is and it's a nice place. You'll get on like a house afire. Well I mean, it's the older one's who find it difficult."

"I know, I'm lucky." The bitter sarcasm couldn't be stifled.

"Well, so you are," she said. "You could have been disfigured and you're not. You have a good home and parents who love you, and you can take advantage of every help there is—and nowadays there's plenty. You're not a lost section of the community anymore. Have you been out yet, on your own?"

"Yes. I can get myself as far as the mailbox and back—with the old white stick, of course." The tapping white stick, symbol of the blind man. He hated it but at least it meant he could go the short distances he knew on his own—to mail a letter, to stretch his legs around the block—but not into High Street. For that he had to wait for his mother or his father, or for the arm of a friend. He was beginning to realize, too, what a difference this was making in their lives as well. Just when they might have expected to be free, here they were saddled with him as if he were a child again: a child who wasn't going to grow beyond their help and attention.

"You'll get more adventurous," she said. "That'll be your trouble."

He was a long way from being that. Imagination played too big a part—the thought of a bicycle catching you as you stepped out into the road, a car mowing you down. When he thought of the hazards he began to sweat.

"Let's talk about you," he said.

"I have exams coming up," she told him.

She was a bit older than he had thought, his own age in fact. When she wasn't living in the nurses' home she stayed in Sussex with her favorite aunt and uncle, not far from the sea. "When I retire I'll live there, too," she said, as if retirement was just around the corner. "It's quiet and peaceful, really fresh fresh air, the downs there to walk over—and on the other side, the sea. After London it's just like another world."

She had a future, could look forward and plan. If things had been different . . . He said, "What do you look like?"

"Oh—fair," she said. "Five foot nothing. Be fat if I didn't watch it. Nothing to write home about."

"You have a nice voice," he said. It was light and easy to listen to—and it chuckled when she wasn't being official. "And you know how to handle patients. You'll pass the exams, all right."

"I'm not so sure about that, but yes—I think I'll pass the exams," she said without any false modesty. "Well, I've lived and thought nothing else . . . since . . ." She didn't finish the sentence. "If I don't pass I don't deserve to be a nurse."

"You knew how to handle me," Roley said. "You got me over those first few days, anyway."

"Oh, well—I'd made that trip myself. It wasn't too difficult to know how you were feeling."

"All the same, I'm not very proud of myself," Roley said. "I'm kicking all the time and I can't help it, and

I can't bear everyone being sorry for me and yet if they weren't I'd resent that, too."

"I know exactly," Susan said. "They don't know how lucky they are, all of them. They don't appreciate what they've got—but then we didn't appreciate it, either. We took it all for granted. It's human nature. The only solution for us is to make something of ourselves. When I've passed my exams and I'm a real nurse I'll think I'm a real person again. You'll feel the same when you've made the grade."

"It is a bit different," Roley said.

"Yes—you have a tougher job, but I think you're a tougher person than I am. You've got to work your way through this stage, there isn't any way you can bypass it—unless you're a saint, and thank goodness you aren't or I'd have detested you."

He hated it when she made a move to go.

"I must—I have homework. But walk me down the road—if you'd like to."

He parted from her reluctantly and walked back, slowly, up the hill. Easy when he was with her to think he could rise to her challenge but now that she had gone all the sickening frustration came flooding back. With her, mentally, he had skipped all the obstacles which were before him, but they were still there to be overcome on his own.

He come to a standstill at the edge of the pavement by the mailbox, feeling with his stick for the curb. This was where he crossed, no problem on this his own quiet road—but quick steps sounded behind him and at the same moment a hand touched his elbow.

"Can I take you across?"

He began to say, "Thank you, I'm fine—"

"I say," the voice said and there was a note of disbelief in it, "I must have got it wrong—but for a moment I thought you looked like—someone I knew . . ." The words tailed off apologetically: "A guy called . . . Rolandson."

Roley turned to face the voice and knew it instantly. It was the last voice he'd heard before—He took a deep breath while memory swept through his brain, leaving it clear and free. "That's right," he said evenly. "Roley Rolandson. And you're Steven Lawrance." He added, cryptically, "I picked up an ear for voices. It's something you develop pretty quickly." He could have told him of other things you developed: sense of smell, and eyes in your fingertips—after you'd made a few mistakes, of course.

"What happened, for heaven's sake?" Steven's voice was shocked. "There wasn't anything wrong when we did the postal service. You'd got a good Christmas coming up."

"No—I was just fine, and then you handed me that parcel." Funny how when Constable Sutton had questioned him there'd been nothing to remember—except the dog pouncing and the explosion. Now the sound of a familiar voice and it was all there.

"Parcel?"

It was clear Steven didn't know what he was talking about—but now it was coming back to him, too.

"Wait a minute, though: it was my last delivery. We walked as far as Park Road together. No, not Park

Road, Park Place. The Gables. I gave you a parcel to return because you were going near there. What's the parcel got to do with it?"

"Everything," Roley said. "I was wondering what was inside, wasn't I? Well, I found out." He made a move to cross the road and Steven moved with him. The white stick poked a little ahead of them, cautiously. "Actually I'm all right on my own around here," he told Steven. "From mailbox to left-hand side of the Crescent, follow around to the next mailbox and into Heath View. I live at the third house on the same side, the one with the privet hedge topping the wall. Easy. I haven't ventured into the town on my own yet, though." He tried to kill the sarcasm by overlaying it with a grim determination.

But Steven was only half listening, his mind still on the parcel, not understanding. "You mean—you opened it?"

Roley shook his head. "No, I didn't have to. The professor keeps a dog. He jumped me. I dropped it—and the thing exploded."

"It was a bomb!" There was unbelief in Steven's voice because you only read about things like that in books or in the papers.

"It was one of his own inventions—backfiring. Only he didn't get it, I did."

"You mean—he sent explosive material through the mail? He must be crazy."

"He's denying it, of course, but they haven't been able to pin it on anyone else yet."

They had come level with Steven's own home and

Roley felt the slight hesitation. "This where you live? I'm fine, really. Don't come any farther."

"But I'd like to," Steven said. "Only, I'll leave my bag first. I'm just back from Cornwall. I spent Christmas there—which I suppose is why I hadn't heard about it." He came back to Roley and walked on with him. "Is it going to get better?" he asked.

Roley shook his head. "No, I really bought it, chum."

"But what about . . ." Steven couldn't finish what he'd been going to say.

"Dr. Roland Rolandson? He's had it," Roley finished for him, and added, as he had said to Susan: "I don't suppose he'd have been any good anyway."

They walked on in silence. Roley could feel Steven's discomfort, his searching for words to express what he felt.

But in a moment the boy said, "Gosh, that was my parcel. I mean, if I hadn't handed it to you, if I hadn't asked you . . ."

"I must admit that did occur to me," Roley said, and couldn't help adding: "It's quite a thought, isn't it?" His white stick seemed to tap out and underline the awful implication and then just as swiftly Roley said, "How were you to know what you were handing me? It might just as easily have been the other way around." And echoing Susan: "Kicking against it doesn't change anything. This is the way it is and that's that."

"Gosh," Steven said again. "I don't know what to say. I only hope that crackpot gets what he deserves.

How can he deny he had anything to do with it if he sent it in the first place?"

"It seems he didn't send it: at least that's his story to the police. We'll be suing him though, or the Post Office if it really didn't come from him."

"No, you can't sue the Post Office. That's like suing the Crown. I'm going in for Law. At least I know that much."

"It's up to the police, then, to find out who did send it. They came around to see me while I was in the hospital but I couldn't tell them anything. Actually, until you stopped me I'd forgotten all about your handing it to me."

"I'd better go in and see them," Steven said, "but there's nothing I can add. It was just handed to me as a return. It was pretty cunning of whomever did send it, wasn't it? Address the parcel incorrectly with your victim's name and address on it as the sender, and let the Post Office do the delivering for you."

"You've got to hate someone pretty strongly to think that up," Roley said.

"It's not as foolproof as it sounds," Steven said. "The remains of the bomb and the wrapping are a give-away—as long as they weren't destroyed."

"The police salvaged everything there was to be salvaged but it hasn't got them very far yet." As good as his word Constable Sutton had been around again, keeping Roley in the picture. "It was a small home-made time bomb—not calculated to kill, they said, but strong enough to cause 'bodily harm.' Nice friends the professor keeps."

"You'd think he'd have some suspicions, all the same," Steven said.

"There's a wide field to choose from," Roley said. "All the professor's inventions are anti-burglar, anti-crook devices. Check on all those and you've got a life's work on your hands."

"No, not really," Steven contradicted him. "However smart a criminal thinks he is, he always leaves some clue that can be traced back to him. The label, for instance—"

"It was typewritten," Roley reminded him. "I remember that much."

"That's right." Steven's voice registered something more than agreement. "And there was something about that typing."

On Constable Sutton's second visit Roley had been able to add that there'd been red sealing wax where the string had been knotted, but now thinking back with Steven he was seeing it again as it had been when Steven had handed the parcel to him.

"I could hardly read the printing it was so faint," he said. "A machine with a worn-out ribbon? Well, there must be thousands of those about."

"No, something else," Steven insisted—and now he was seeing the address on the parcel quite clearly. "It was the o's," he said. "They were out of alignment. They were all just a fraction lower than all the other letters. It stuck out because there were a lot of them."

"Yes, you're right." The mental picture of the dropped o's was suddenly plain and as clear in Roley's mind as if he had been back again in the dark, frost-bound street, peering down at the writing on the label. He said, "I thought I'd told Constable Sutton all I knew, but I wouldn't have remembered that if you hadn't jogged my memory. I think someone's got to take a look now at the professor's typewriter and see if that's out of alignment, too."

They had come to Roley's second mailbox, the one at the end of the Crescent. Steven was beginning to cross over the road but Roley was hanging back. Steven heard it then, the stutter of a motorcycle engine, coming louder, nearer, until it swung around the corner of the Crescent and swept past them and away out of sight. "I used to fancy myself riding one of those," Roley said, as they crossed together. "Now the sound of them sends me into a cold sweat."

"You heard it before I did, all the same," Steven said, marveling.

"Do my ears look bigger than they did? You wouldn't know but that's the way it feels. Without them I really would be sunk."

They walked on a few yards in silence and then Steven said, "If I can do anything for you—any time. I'm near enough and I'd be glad to."

"That's what you all say. God, how I hate it!" The outburst was instinctive and violent, rage bubbling up inside needing only a word of sympathy to explode it, but in a moment Roley had recovered himself. "I'm sorry, I didn't mean to fly at you. It's just depending on everyone for almost everything you want, never being able to dash out and do it for yourself—unless it's around the houses like this. People are marvelous— but they stop treating you like a human being. They don't mean to, but it stands to reason you're not going anywhere so if they're late coming for you what does it matter? Or if they can't make it at all, another time will do just as well. You just don't count anymore—as a person. That's what gets you more than anything else."

"Well—I'd like to come and talk even if you didn't want anything," Steven said.

"And I'd like you to," Roley said. "Now, let's talk about you."

6   *Constable Sutton Makes a Comment*

After that Roley had a visit from Steven most weekends, the weekends he was home from the Braille school. Sometimes—most times—Susan was there, too. Steven liked her. She was attractive, he thought, and with plenty of spirit—as when Roley had introduced them.

"Oh—you two haven't met," he'd said. "Steven meet Susan: Susan Lambert. She talked a lot of sense to me when I was in hospital. I'm her good deed."

"You're nothing of the sort," Susan had answered

hotly. "I don't do anything I don't want to do and you can believe that or not, just as you please."

It was a shame, Steven had thought, that Roley couldn't see the flashing look she shot him and the quick color that had rushed to her cheeks. Bridging the angry moment he said, "I went down to the police station the other night and said my piece. They took my fingerprints and asked a lot of questions about the sorter who handed me the parcel. I felt like a criminal. Fortunately it all tallied with what they already knew. They were pleased, though, with what I remembered about the writing on the label." He explained to Susan and went on. "It seems the professor had been receiving threatening letters—typewritten—and the o's in the letters were just the same as they were on the label, a fraction below all the other letters."

"So what?" Roley said.

"The same character who sent the letters sent the parcel."

"And that leaves them just exactly where they were before."

"Oh, you can be the most infuriating person!" Susan exploded. "If it wasn't for the fact—" She stopped as if her tongue had been chopped off.

"—that I'm blind?" Roley prompted her. "Don't mind me, I'm getting used to it."

Susan's eyes were full of tears, her teeth biting on her lower lip. She hadn't meant to say anything, hadn't known the words were even there until they had leapt out. Steven tried to think of something to say that would show he understood and was sympathetic without seeming to criticize Roley, but at that moment

Mrs. Rolandson came in. She carried a tray of coffee and sandwiches and Susan jumped up to help her before Steven had collected himself.

"Now you've all met, that's nice," she said, and to Steven: "You're one of my husband's pupils, Roley tells me."

"Not a very bright one, I'm afraid," Steven said. "I enjoy his classes, though."

"And you're going in for Law. I think you must be *very* bright."

"My father isn't very happy about it. He's an architect and hoped I'd follow in his footsteps, but he's got used to the idea now."

"Well, that's the way it often goes," Roley's mother said. "No one's been a doctor in this family—as far as anyone knows—but it was all Roley wanted to do."

Softly spoken as they were, the words were like a thunderclap in the room. Steven floundered miserably in the little silence that gripped them all and finally managed, "I feel terrible about it. The parcel was given to me to deliver. I'd no right to have passed it on."

"Oh, don't feel like that about it," Mrs. Rolandson said. "No one's blaming you. No one's blaming anyone except the one who sent it. It's happened and we've got to make the best of it."

"*I've* got to make the best of it," Roley corrected her.

"That's right," his mother said. She put the cup of coffee she had poured out into his hands. "We're all very proud of you, darling. You're miles ahead of the others with the Braille."

"Excuse me if I can't work up too much enthusiasm about that," Roley said.

That was one of Roley's bad days and although it had been embarrassing and saddening it had welded the three of them closer together.

Getting to know Roley's father better had been something else Steven was enjoying. He'd admired him as a teacher. Apart from teaching the language he had managed to give the class a vivid picture of the country, the Italy he himself had known as a boy and not the colorful, glamorous one of the tourist abroad. He based his lessons on his own experiences there and on actual daily living.

Characteristically he had greeted Steven: *"Bon giorno,* Steven. *Come va?"*

Steven had managed to keep up with him for a few moments and then had lapsed into English.

"You really are good," Roley said, impressed.

"Your father's a fine teacher," Steven said.

"You'd had a good grounding at school before I caught you," Mr. Rolandson said. "And at your age you can learn anything fast. Look at Roley with Braille. The aptitude is there too, I know, but a young, alert mind can absorb so much."

There was only eager interest in Mr. Rolandson's voice, no undertones of the tragedy that had struck them, no suggestion of the bitter disappointment it was for all of them. A large Braille tome was open on the small table at Roley's knee and Steven went over to look at it. Raised dots on a blank page, more than anything else it reminded him of Morse code he'd learned when he was in the Boy Scouts.

"As a matter of fact it poses an interesting question," Mr. Rolandson said, "like what came first, the chicken or the egg? Morse was the invention of an American artist who lived from 1791 to 1872. Louis Braille, a Frenchman, was born a little later but in that same period. He was himself blind from the age of three, became a teacher of the blind and invented this method of reading by touch." He ran a finger along a line of Roley's book. "Raised dots in various combinations of numbers and positions. But there was someone else, born a little earlier than either of them—Valentin Hauy. He was a teacher of the blind, too, and thought up characters embossed on paper. In 1784 he established an institute for the blind in Paris. So your guess is as good as mine as to who really did invent it."

"The important thing," Roley's mother said, "is that it was invented, but Monsieur Braille does seem to have collected a lot of the credit."

"There's a story attached to Hauy that he gave a coin to a blind beggar and that the beggar called after him, drawing his attention to the value of the coin, thinking his benefactor must have made a mistake. Hauy, knowing the man to be totally blind, asked him how he had been able to identify the coin so quickly and the man replied that it was sufficient for him to pass his finger over it. That's supposed to be the origin of Hauy's invention."

"And there's the story of the domino," Mrs. Rolandson reminded him, "that was supposed to have prompted Louis Braille to invent his method."

"A grain of truth in all the stories, I expect," Roley's father said. "It's an ingenious method, all the same, and it hasn't stopped there. There's a Braille type-writer. I saw work done on one at the school where Roley is and I can tell you it was a better piece of work than most sighted people would turn out."

It was left to Constable Sutton, several weeks after that, to come up with another really exciting scheme for the blind. He had made a habit of calling in every now and again when he came off duty on weekends. Sometimes there was a crumb of news to add to the other scattered crumbs of news that didn't seem to lead anywhere, but suddenly this one looked as if it was going to—

"There was a fingerprint on the sealing wax," he told Roley, "and they've identified the owner of it."

"It's taken long enough," Roley couldn't help saying. "I thought the police kept files of them."

"So they do—in stations all over the country," Constable Sutton told him patiently. "We'd circulated this one in the usual way and Manchester has come up with the owner. A man calling himself Charlie Phelps, petty crimes, handbag snatching, that sort of thing. This means he must have moved south and is in business down here. It's only a question of time now before we pull him in."

"He's gotten a bit more ambitious, hasn't he?" Roley said.

"It could be retaliation—against the professor for interfering in a lucrative career. I mean, if he'd come up against some of the professor's anti-crook devices he might think it a good idea to put him out of business."

"I suppose that does make sense," Roley said. "It isn't going to do me any good, though."

"No, but it's a game that must be stopped. So long as he's at large he can try it again. We've put a watch on the professor's house. He's got the jitters and I don't wonder. How's the reading going?" he asked.

"Not bad," Roley said. "The books aren't exactly portable, though."

Constable Sutton picked up the book resting on Roley's knees. He'd never seen one before. It was heavy and bulky and as Roley said, not exactly portable.

"I don't really mind that," Roley said. "When I've mastered it it's going to mean I'm not dependent on someone reading to me. I wish I could say the same for going out."

"What you need is a dog," Constable Sutton said.

"A dog?"

"Yes, a Guide Dog. One of those would take you anywhere you wanted to go at any time you felt like going."

The shock of excitement that shook Roley took him by surprise. Questions rushed to his lips but before they could be spoken, the flaming sword of memory cut them back. As clearly as if it were happening all over again he could feel the sudden impact of the heavy body, hear again the explosion ringing in his ears, see in his mind's eye the blinding flash. "A dog. I couldn't," he gasped.

"He'd be a companion, too," Constable Sutton was saying. "You'd feel like a different person in no time at all."

"I couldn't. I couldn't." Suddenly Roley was shouting and in his voice there was a note almost of terror.

"I say," Constable Sutton looked at him in alarm,

"you don't want to feel like that about it. You can't blame the dog for what happened. How was it to know—"

"It jumped me, didn't it? A brute with no sense—and you're asking me to make a companion of one."

"Those dogs wouldn't jump you. They're trained for their job—taking people like you out into the streets, through traffic, protecting you."

"No, thank you," Roley said. He'd gotten a grip on himself now. "You haven't had the close contact with them that I've had. I wouldn't trust one again as far as I could—" He had been going to say "see it." It was happening all the time, the automatic use of the old turn of phrase that didn't apply anymore.

"Well—you know best," Constable Sutton said, "but it's a shame."

7   *Susan Has an Idea*

"You're wasting your breath," Roley said for the hundredth time.

"And you're cutting off your nose to spite your face," Susan said. "I don't know why I didn't think of Guide Dogs myself. It's the perfect answer."

"They'd send one of their men down to talk to you about them," Steven said. "You wouldn't have to commit yourself but at least listen to what they've got to say."

"No," Roley said, "and now let's drop it, shall we? There's some more news about the parcel. I'm more interested in that."

"You mean—they've found out who sent it?" Susan exclaimed.

"No, but the trail's getting warm. The police interviewed the professor again and—what d'you know? Looking through his papers they found some typewritten ones with the o's out of alignment."

"He did send it, then?" Steven couldn't keep the excitement out of his voice.

"No, but it seems his typewriter had been out of order—dropping the o's—and at the end of last year he'd sent it to be repaired, just before the threatening letters began to arrive. That's why the police hadn't been on to it before; the typewriter had had a complete new set of keys."

"That sounds fishy, if you ask me," Steven said.

"The police thought so, too," Roley said, "so they went to the shop who'd repaired it—the Stationers and Printers in High Street. They went through the books back to the time the professor's typewriter was in and found that a chap calling himself George Tate had worked on it but had left immediately after he'd done that job."

"George Tate?"

"Well, it isn't likely Charlie Phelps would have used his own name after planting a time bomb in the area, is it?"

"No—but until you find George Tate and check his fingerprints against those of Charlie Phelps you're back where you started."

"No, not quite," Constable Sutton told him. "We've got a physical description of him now as well: one that tallies pretty well with the one from Manchester.

About five foot ten, fair curly hair, fresh complexion, good-looking in a flashy, cocky sort of way. It looks as if the professor's in the clear anyway."

"In the clear but not feeling very comfortable, I bet," Steven said.

"He'll be all right," Roley agreed with the Constable. "The police have put a watch on the house." And added as the policeman had: "Charlie Phelps' little game needs stopping before he kills someone."

They talked about Steven, then. The university he was attending was near enough for him to be a non-resident, but he might live in next year. "You get more out of it," he said. "Just when arguments and discussions are warming up, we characters have to pack up and head home." He was enjoying it, though.

It was a world quite foreign to Roley and Susan and they listened fascinated to Steven's talk about the Inns of Court, which are the direct descendants of the schools of law in the Middle Ages. How, now that he had been accepted, he must "keep Terms." There were four of these Terms a year and he must keep twelve of them. It was so archaic it wasn't true, but its roots in ancient history was what made it so marvelous. As a student he had to dine three times in Hall during each of the Terms. At each table there were four of you and this formed your "mess." You talked to no one outside your own table! You relaxed, drank ale, wine, or cider, and talked shop. "Well, after all, the Inns were hostelries in the Middle Ages and this keeps up the tradition. I think it's great. In a way it's—it's what gives English Law it's weight."

"You're spoiling the picture of my own job for me,"

Susan told him. "I can only go back as far as Florence Nightingale. Doesn't it seem incredible that nursing didn't have any proper status until she got it organized —less than a hundred years ago? And talking about going back, I'll never be up in the morning if I don't go—right now."

But home and in bed Susan couldn't get to sleep for thinking—not about Steven and his Inns of Court, but, about the idea of a Guide Dog for Roley. And next morning, no matter what she was doing, it kept coming back to her. Finally, in a tea break, she went down to the Matron's office and looked in the telephone directory. There it was—Guide Dogs for the Blind Association, Uxbridge Road. That was the other side the river, a bus ride away but not too far. She'd go there on her day off, have a talk with somebody, see if they couldn't come up with some suggestion for getting around Roley's resistance.

The office was in a large block of a modern building standing back from the busy main suburban road. The elevator had whisked her up to the fourth floor and deposited her facing the open door before she had made up her mind what she was going to say. A young woman sitting at a desk looked up and said, "May I help you?"

"Oh—I wanted to speak to someone—about Guide Dogs—for someone," she blurted out clumsily.

"Take a seat a moment," the young woman said, indicating a chair, "and I'll see if Mr. Welby can see you. He's only just come in but I know his next appointment isn't until three o'clock." She turned and went through a door into an inner room and after a few moments came back again. "Yes, he'll see you. You're lucky. Usually he's booked right up."

"I'm sorry—I should have telephoned you first," Susan apologized to the man standing smilingly to greet her beside a piled-up desk. "I didn't really think about seeing anyone in particular—just asking for a friend."

"Well, I think I may be able to help you better than anyone else," Mr. Welby said, and moved a chair up to the desk for her.

He was about the same age her father would have been if he hadn't died, Susan thought—and not unlike him with his dark brindled hair and heavy horn-rimmed glasses; about the same height and build, too.

Mr. Welby was easy to talk to and surprisingly he didn't think Roley's attitude strange. "I'm quite sure if the same thing had happened to us we would be taking a very poor view of dogs, too, but I do agree a dog is the answer for a boy that age. It would give him back his freedom and make him independent of others, and you as a nurse will appreciate the psychological effect of that. Give him exercise, too, that he wouldn't otherwise get; be very good for him. On the other hand, it won't work at all unless he has a change of attitude. The student must *want* and appreciate a dog like this. They're carefully picked in the first place and then they're highly trained. They're as sensitive as you or I to the way people feel about them."

"But if we could get around that"—Susan didn't know how, but it had to be managed, somehow—"could he have one?"

"One of our trainers would have to visit your friend

first," Mr. Welby said. "A lot of technical details have to be gone into apart from finding out if the student is a suitable subject to have a dog. A report from his doctor, and personal details collected so that the right size dog can be balanced against the student's own height and weight; how active he is and what kind of a job the dog will be required to do. It matters very much matching the right dog with the right person."

"You have plenty, though," Susan assumed.

"No, unfortunately we haven't. There are always more customers waiting than we have dogs. We have young ones coming along all the time, of course, but there are never enough to go around."

"How do you mean—coming along?" Susan said. Surely all one had to do was buy lots of puppies and train them?

"It isn't as easy as you think," Mr. Welby said. "For instance, only certain breeds of dogs will do. Mainly we use Labradors in this country, and German shepherds or Alsatians, and some collies. They're the right size. So to begin with, that cuts out a lot of otherwise good, teachable dogs. And then the puppies have to be carefully selected: they must be physically fit and free from nerves and no tendency to aggression. Even so, all of them don't make the grade."

"It's more complicated than I thought," Susan said.

"And of course the dogs that are chosen can't begin to be used until they're mature. We have what we call Puppy Walkers into whose homes the puppies go to be house trained and where they get their first training in obedience, so that finally they come to us ready to start their further training as a guide. And that takes three months under experts who know exactly the hazards and difficulties a dog is going to meet in his task of guiding a blind person."

"I'd no idea," Susan said, fascinated, "all that going on. Somehow one doesn't think."

"Well, that's natural, too," Mr. Welby said. "It isn't until we're brought up against a reality like blindness—or any other disability for that matter—that we start thinking about what there is that will help."

"And then we're not really interested unless it's happened to someone we . . ." The words trailed off as she caught Mr. Welby's glance. The color rose to her cheeks and she ended, lamely, ". . . Someone we know. Could there be a dog for Roley?" she added quickly. "Could someone go and see him and try to make him see sense?"

Mr. Welby smiled. "We do try to help," he said. "Let me think about it for a few days. Maybe I'll come up with an idea. Another thing we try to make sure of," he said, "is that we're not beaten."

8   *Constable Sutton Weighs In*

Susan didn't dare tell Roley what she had done but she told Steven. "Well, I had to do something," she said in answer to Steven's look of astonishment?—admiration? She didn't know what the look was but the news really had shaken him.

"And I just talked," he said, "and blew my top. Good for you."

"If it works," she reminded him. "I just thought that the Guide Dog people were the ones to convince him if anyone could. If they can't I don't see what else we can do."

"He's got to be saved from himself," Steven agreed.

"I mean, quite apart from a dog helping him to get around on his own, this obsession against them ought to be broken. If it isn't, it's going to grow into something that will rule his whole life—like not visiting people who own one, or not letting anyone with a dog visit him, and eventually not going out in case he meets one. It's mentally bad. It's unhealthy."

The following weekend Susan called in to see Roley half expecting to be confronted by a furious tirade, but the atmosphere was as usual—welcoming and friendly. It was certain he was quite oblivious to anything going on. Actually he was entirely wrapt up in his efforts to master Braille. He read long passages aloud to Susan and there wasn't any doubt of the progress he was making. His fingers moved so much faster over the pages and only rarely did he stumble or go back to correct himself. If only he could be persuaded to put the same energy and determination into wanting the freedom he could so easily have with a dog, she thought sadly.

The next time she was there, the doorbell rang a moment after she arrived. In a panic she started to get to her feet.

"Don't go," Roley pleaded with her. "It won't be anyone—unless it's Steven."

It wasn't Steven but it wasn't anyone from the Association, either. It was Constable Sutton.

"I haven't any news for you," he apologized, "but I was just passing. Am I barging in?" he asked.

"No, of course not. You know Nurse Lambert." Roley had come to look on the constable as a friend. The man never brought with him the one bit of news he was wanting to hear, but he was good company with his tales about his job. He'd lost the embarrassment and awkwardness Roley couldn't help sensing those first days in hospital, but maybe that was because he himself was getting used to his blindness and was back in normal surroundings.

The constable pulled up a chair between Susan and Roley. "Charlie Phelps is giving us a real run for our money. As a matter of fact I thought there would be some news for you this visit. The Printers and Stationers came up with an address—Harvey Cottages. Number 22."

"Where's that?" Roley asked. He'd lived in Barnwood all his life—*and* helped with the mail delivery in most parts of the town—but he hadn't heard of Harvey Cottages.

"Back end of the town, down by the railway sidings," Constable Sutton told him. "It's a poor part and off my normal beat. I haven't been down there in months, but I didn't waste any time getting there, I promise you, and there they were—dingy little houses, blackened by smoke from the railway and crumbling with decay—and all of them empty. Up for demolition. He'd given a phony address along with the phony name, unless the cottages were occupied at the time Charlie was in the repair shop."

"In which case the town hall must have a record of where the people living there moved to," Roley said.

"We worked on that one," the constable said, "and accounted for everyone—except Charlie."

"People aren't very observant," Susan said. She knew that from accident cases that came into hospital—half of them couldn't describe anything, or recognize a description when you gave it to them. "If you've only got fingerprints to go on and the color of his hair and eyes, couldn't they have seen him without knowing he was the one you're looking for?"

"That's what we're up against," Constable Sutton agreed. "He could have disguised himself a bit, had a haircut, or dyed it. They're up to all the tricks."

"That's right," Roley said. "Supposing he doesn't look like his description anymore? I mean, supposing he isn't disguised—but *disfigured*? Well, you said yourself the parcel could have been retaliation."

"Yeah." The constable nodded thoughtfully. "I was thinking of it being retaliation against the professor's anti-crook devices, trying to warn him off, but it could be he'd actually come up against one of the devices himself, been hurt by one of them. It's a thought."

"I'm sure Roley's right," Susan said excitedly. "It's so obvious, someone ought to have thought about it before."

"It's often the obvious that trips you up," the constable said. "The answer to any problem is there staring you in the face but we're usually too busy looking around for a clever setup."

"It could be all you're looking for and this as well," Roley said. He felt rather pleased with himself, it seemed so natural: if you'd been hurt yourself you wanted to hurt back. It was the way he felt about the whole canine race. It left a lot of loopholes, though: like, how did Charlie Phelps alias George Tate know that the professor's typewriter was going to come into the shop for repair?

"When we do get the answer it'll look so simple we'll be kicking ourselves we haven't seen it all along," Constable Sutton said. He added in a moment: "Have you thought any more about those dogs? You should, you know. They'd open up a new world for you, really they would."

"Do you mind?" Roley said. "I thought I'd made it clear I'm not interested in dogs."

"But if you saw what they can do," Constable Sutton persisted, ignoring Roley's belligerent tone. "I had to take a man to our Police Dog Training school yesterday. Those animals are fabulous."

"Alsatians," Susan said, anticipating him. "I've seen them patrolling around here. I agree they look absolutely marvelous but too much like wolves for my liking."

Constable Sutton said, "There's no truth, you know, in the tale that an Alsatian has a strain of wolf in him. He's gentle and trustworthy and so intelligent it isn't believable—but old tales die hard and just by the way he looks, without anything else, an Alsatian can intimidate a would-be crook, and often that's all that's needed."

"He'd intimidate me, all right," Susan said. "I wouldn't go within a mile of one."

"They're taught to hold, not to attack," Constable Sutton told her, "and they're not only used to track down criminals, they're used in searching for missing persons."

"Can't we change the subject?" Roley said.

"No, we can't." Susan turned on him. "Just because you're blind doesn't entitle you to any special consider-

ation. Well, that's what you're always saying. You want
to be treated just like everybody else. So—I want to
hear about those dogs, and if you don't you'll just have
to not listen for five minutes."

"O.K., I'm sorry," Roley apologized grudgingly. He
wanted it both ways, he knew that: to be able to moan
and kick about himself and at the same time not made
to feel different from anyone else. He minded, too,
what Susan thought.

"They were in the middle of a class when I got
there," Constable Sutton went on, as if there'd been
no interruption. "What those dogs can do is just nobody's business. To watch them pick up a scent—
although other cross-tracks have been laid—ignore the
new track and keep to the original scent is pretty
marvelous. I watched the agility training, too. It was
like a blessed circus, seeing them clear obstacles—low
ones at first and gradually the trainer increases the
height and the length until the dog is clearing an
obstacle which is really too high for it to clear. That's
the staggering part about it—to see a dog leap up
several feet short of the top of a wall and because of
its great muscle power it's able to pull itself up and
over. And not only that, but on landing on the other
side it'll stand and wait until it's given the order to go
forward by its handler. They're more human than
human beings. You have to respect them."

"Respect them and keep your distance," Roley
couldn't resist adding. "Well, that's the idea, isn't it?
Terrify the victim into submission."

"These are police dogs," Constable Sutton reminded
him. "Guide Dogs have a very different training—but

what they have in common is intelligence. If they're chosen carefully and trained properly a dog can do just about anything, it seems to me."

"O.K.," Roley said. "You've made your point. Next time I'll make sure the dog's fully trained before I let it attack me."

There wasn't anything you could do for him, Susan thought miserably. He was going to let it ruin the rest of his life.

9   *Steven Blows His Top*

Two more weeks went by. Susan saw Roley at the Braille school and at weekends at his home, but there was still no mention of any word from the Guide Dog people.

"Mr. Welby was so nice, too," Susan told Steven as they walked up to Roley's together one Friday evening. "I was quite sure he meant to do something. The usual procedure is to send a trainer around to see what the position is; if the blind person is capable of handling a dog, if he's old enough, or maybe too old— that sort of thing. He agreed that Roley sounded the kind of person who should have a dog, but you see, nothing's happened."

"Getting around Roley's opposition is a pretty tough assignment." Steven tried to console her. "And from what you've said about the whole setup, they must be up to their necks trying to fix up people who really *do* want a dog without thinking out ways and means of forcing someone to want one.

"But the longer time goes on the more set Roley becomes on this dog-hate thing. Now you can't get him even to talk about them. You should have heard him the other evening when Constable Sutton wanted to tell us about the police dogs."

"I was there," Susan reminded him.

"Yes, of course you were. Well, he nearly went off the deep end. And yet he'd be the first to argue someone into doing something if he thought it was going to do him some good. He ought to be made to snap out of it, somehow."

"We're back to 'but how?' again," Susan said despondently.

Roley's mother answered the door. "Oh, I am glad you've come," she greeted them. "I'm not having a very successful day."

"Why, what's wrong?" Susan asked her.

Mrs. Rolandson lowered her voice. "I forgot to get tickets for the Festival Hall concert tomorrow night, and now they're booked up. Roley is convinced I forgot because he doesn't matter anymore; and I moved something out of its usual place and he fell over it; and a school friend who was coming to see him this

morning didn't turn up. We're all in the doghouse."
She laughed.

"Oh, poor you," Susan sympathized. "I'm sorry
about the friend and the fall—but maybe I can do
something about the tickets. Hospitals often get com-
plimentaries."

"Oh, if you could that would be wonderful. He'll
be glad to see you two, anyway."

Roley may have been glad but he wasn't going to
show it. "I'd have thought you two would have something better to do," was his greeting.

"Well, we did look down the movie list but there's
nothing on worth seeing," Steven told him cheerfully.
"And it's too cold for a walk. We said, let's go to
Roley's, there'll be a good fire there and a comfortable
chair."

"But not very good company," Roley said.

"That's all right," Susan assured him lightly. "Don't
you mind us, we'll do the talking and you can listen—
if you're interested. In any case I want to hear how
Steven's making out with Law."

But Steven couldn't keep it up. "I want to hear how
Roley's doing, first," he said.

"Oh, I'm getting by," Roley said. "No one has to
worry about me."

The false brightness should have warned them—
that and the heavy sarcasm—but Susan went on:

"We're not worried about you. I think you know so
exactly what's good for you that you'll get on like a
house afire. Steven isn't so sure of himself. He's willing
to try his new classes before condemning them out of
hand."

"Bully for him," Roley said. "Perhaps I should try the basket weaving, then. You know, I think I might be good at that. Number One blind basket weaver. I could have a plate on the door—in place of the doctor's plate I might have had in Harley Street. I could start with a dog basket. That would be appropriate, wouldn't it?"

"Excuse me if I don't laugh," Steven said. "I don't think you're being particularly funny."

"All right—no dog baskets," Roley promised. "I could do a line in chairs, instead. If you've any at home with the bottoms out you'd be able to bring them over."

"Stop it!" Susan shouted him down. "I accept all you say about why you won't have a Guide Dog. Perhaps I'd feel the same—though I hope I'd have the guts to give it a try. But you can still train for a medical job. Hundreds of blind people become physiotherapists."

"I seem to have heard that one, too," Roley said, "and you can keep it. Look, I appreciate what you're both trying to do—" The mood was passing but Susan and Steven were too angry to notice. "I guess it's the way I'm made," Roley went on. "I'm not one of your" —he was searching for the word he wanted and at last found it—"well-adjusted characters. That's the word for it nowadays. What it really means is normal and sensible. I'm neither, so let's accept that too."

"I can tell you what we've evidently got to accept," Steven said, stung to fury at last, "and that is that you're a pig-headed, unreasonable fool, determined to make what's happened to you ruin the rest of your life and everybody else's life around you. No one can give you your sight back but plenty of people can help you if you'll just stop being sorry for yourself and let them. O.K.—go on sitting on your backside, go on tapping your way around the houses with your little white stick. I'm stuffed with you"—he gave himself a slap under the chin—"right up to here. Good night." He was up and out of his chair, had crossed the room and opened the door and slammed it behind him before the other two could draw a breath to stop him. In a moment the front door slammed.

Susan said into the silence that filled the room, "Well—he really told you, didn't he?"

"Yeah, yeah—he told me all right," Roley said. There was no sarcasm in his voice now; all the false brightness was gone. Suddenly Susan was desperately sorry for him. She'd been sorry before, but this was different. This was like seeing someone's soul stripped bare, someone who'd already lost so much. She said softly, "He didn't mean it."

"I think he did," Roley said. "He's right, too. Every word he said was right."

Silence fell again, but before it became unsupportable Susan said, "About the Festival Hall concert. I think I can get tickets through the hospital."

"Music to soothe the savage breast," Roley said, making an effort to recapture the old atmosphere.

"I'd like to go myself," Susan said. "I didn't know you were fond of music—real music."

"Mother isn't really keen. She was only going to please me." Roley's voice was eager and hopeful.

"Why don't I try to get three," Susan said, "then we

could ask Steven, too, and your mother can do something she really likes."

"If you think Steven would come," Roley said doubtfully.

"I know he'd come. He's really fond of you, Roley— that's why he got so mad. If you don't care especially for anyone, well, they don't arouse you to anything."

"That's psychology, I suppose," Roley said, ruefully. "Well—I hope you're right."

"I know I am, just you leave it to me."

10   *Roley Has a Visitor*

"A concert?" Steven echoed as if Susan had suggested something too terrible to contemplate.

"It's a good concert," Susan told him. "Abner York is the solo pianist. He's fabulous."

"I've never heard of him," Steven said. "That sort of music isn't in my line. Really."

"How much have you heard?"

"Well . . . not any. I make a point of not hearing any."

"Look," Susan said. "As well as being a concert it's an olive branch. Do you or don't you want things right again between you and Roley?"

"Of course I do. Couldn't I just go and say I'm sorry? The moment I got out of the house I really was sorry I'd said what I did."

"No," Susan said, firmly. "If I tell Roley you don't want to come he'll never accept the real reason, he'll be absolutely certain it's because you're furious at him."

"O.K.," Steven said at last. "But I hope you know what you're doing to me. I may never be the same again."

"And that may be truer than you think." Susan laughed. "You may find you like it. Well, as a matter of fact, I took it for granted you would come and I rang Mrs. Rolandson and she said we were to go there for tea first. She and Mr. Rolandson are going to the National Film Theatre which is nearly next door and so they can give us a ride—and bring us home after."

"Couldn't we all have gone to the Film Theatre?" Steven began, hopefully. "O.K., no, I suppose not," he added, quickly catching Susan's eye. "I'll call for you, then—about half past three tomorrow."

All Saturday morning Steven was kicking himself for letting himself in for the ordeal by good music. He wouldn't have minded a Pop session, or even classical jazz—but a Beethoven Concerto and a Haydn Symphony were a lot to ask of anyone. However, he had to agree with Susan that it was a good way of getting back on the old footing with Roley. He'd been a fool to go for him the way he had, as if he himself wouldn't have been much worse if he were in Roley's shoes. It was so easy to tell someone else what best to do. If it had been himself it had happened to, he'd have gone right around the bend and wanted to shoot every dog in sight.

"Except you couldn't even see them to shoot them," Susan reminded him as they walked up to Roley's home together. "That's what you've got to remember all the time. It isn't just something that's going to be a nuisance for a few days or weeks or months, it's for always."

"Yes, of course, you're right," Steven said, humbled by the realization all over again of what it really was meaning for Roley. "And that's what makes it so frustrating when he won't try the one thing that could make it a bit more bearable. But I promise—from now on, dogs as a subject are taboo."

As they came up to the front of the house an upstairs window was opened and Roley's mother called down to them: "The door's open. Roley's been counting the moments for you to come."

"Counting the moments for *you* to come," Steven told Susan as they crossed the hall. "I hope you're right about his being glad to see me."

Roley was sitting in his favorite chair, his face turned toward the door: a face alight with excitement. "Five more minutes and I was going to phone you. You too, Steven." He seemed quite unconscious of the fact that they had parted, less than twenty-four hours before, in a cloud of blue smoke. "I had a visitor this morning," he went on, not giving either of them a chance to interrupt. "You'll never guess in a thousand years. A man called John Morley with his Guide Dog, Jess."

"Guide Dog—?" The expression on Steven's face would have made Roley laugh out loud.

"O.K., so I was wrong. That's what you told me, wasn't it? I've decided to give you the benefit of the doubt and try one."

"Oh, Roley!" Susan's explosion was dangerously close to tears. Having waited weekend after weekend for Roley to hear from the Guide Dog Association it had slipped right out of her mind this last week.

"It's a pity it's got to be a dog, but if it's the only way for me to get about under my own steam I've decided to give it a try. This chap came from Brackley—by train and bus—just himself and the dog. I didn't believe it at first but my mother let him in and it's on the level."

"Well, what do you know?" Steven dropped into the chair opposite Roley. "Here I've been kicking myself for not keeping my big mouth shut. Last night I *really* cut you into bits."

"It was what I needed. Someone ought to have given me the works ages ago," Roley said. "Before the door slammed behind you last night I was beginning to come to my senses, and when you'd gone, Susan, I began to see myself as you were both seeing me."

"Oh, Roley—no," Susan began, but Roley wasn't listening, he was too eager to get them into the picture. "I don't mind telling you I stayed awake most of the night trying to sort myself out. I wasn't sure where I ought to start. And then John Morley walked in."

"And I'd begun to think they weren't going to do anything," Susan marveled. "I should have known Mr.

Welby wasn't the kind of person to let anyone down. He said he'd think of something. I thought he meant he'd send one of the trainers. I wouldn't have thought of one of the Guide Dogs with its master if I'd thought forever."

"It was you then, Susan. I guessed as much when he said a young lady had called at the office. O.K.—well, I'm going to try at least and not let either of you down. I really *am* going to try." He was convincing himself now but they both knew he'd already had out the fight with himself and won it. "He didn't give me a chance to change my mind," Roley went on. "He rang the Training Center—while I sat here. A new course is starting and there's a vacancy. One of the trainers is coming up to see me next week. If I measure up I might be able to go right away."

"Of course you'll measure up." Nothing could go wrong now, Susan was telling herself, nothing, nothing.

"He didn't like my not being a hundred percent for the dog," Roley said. "Well, I had to tell him the way I felt. I can't help it and I can't see myself changing, but I'm prepared to give it a try. If that dog can guide John Morley in and out of trains and on and off buses and bring him through this town to this door, another one like it can do the same for me."

Steven said quickly: "I'm butting in again—but if I were you I wouldn't say too much to the trainer about the way you feel about them. Well, I mean, you want to be given the chance to try."

"Look—I'm entitled to one." The aggression was there again, but not so dangerously near the surface. "Well, I am, aren't I? No one says I've got to be maudlin over the thing—but I'll watch it." Steven was right. The chaps who trained the dogs had a say in handing them out, that's what John Morley had said. He'd worked up enough courage to try it and he didn't now want anyone telling him that he didn't qualify.

"Tell us about the dog," Susan said, fending off the sparks which had looked about to fly.

"It's a Labrador," Roley said, dying to pass on all the information he'd been given, "and a bitch. It seems they're less complicated than dogs. They don't have the same lamppost complex for one thing. And they're not so sexy. And like Constable Sutton's police dogs, once I'm allocated one she moves in and lives with me, day and night." It was one of the bits—one of the many bits—he didn't like but he wasn't going to think about it too much at this stage.

"How long will you have to stay at the Center?" Steven asked him. The ice was still thin and the best thing was to let Roley skate on it alone.

"A course lasts a month and before that it's taken three months to train the dogs. And what do you think it costs? 250 pounds."

"Is that what you'll have to pay?" Susan hadn't thought about the cost, but now she was thinking that a blind person, robbed of a salaried job, was less likely than most people to be able to afford as much as that.

"No, as a matter of fact you're only asked for a donation—as much as you feel you can afford—and as far as I can make out, the main idea of that is so you'll feel the dog is really yours. It's pretty good, isn't it? All that money being raised voluntarily. People collect silver paper and milk bottle tops—that brings them in quite a bit of money too."

"I'll never throw another one away as long as I live," Susan said. "I must have lost the Center hundreds of dogs."

"Funny how little you know about a thing," Steven said, "until you get interested yourself in it. I've probably passed dozens of Guide Dogs without noticing them."

"I doubt it," Roley said. "It hasn't been going so long in this country, so John Morley said—and most of that time's been spent building the scheme up. And it started in America, a woman called Dorothy Eustis and her husband. They'd had an Alsatian that could do just about anything and that started them thinking."

"Go on, it sounds fascinating," Steven said. Whatever Roley felt about dogs he was at least interested now in the movement, and that was going to go a long way toward helping him adjust to such a new way of life.

"Well," Roley went on, "they had to go to live in Switzerland, and found themselves living close to the German border, and near where some Alsatians were working as frontier guards with the police. As a matter of fact, the first dogs they trained were for police work. Then one day the husband was in Potsdam and saw dogs working with blinded ex-servicemen—and that was it as far as Dorothy Eustis was concerned. Why not train dogs to help all blind people?"

"I'd like to point out—in case you haven't noticed— that it took a woman to think of a humane use for them," Susan interposed.

"O.K.," Roley laughed, "but the husband was around, too, don't forget—and they might not have been able to do any of it alone. They had a friend back home in the States, a man called Elliot Humphrey. They persuaded him to join them and that's when it really began: the research, and the training, and the breeding. Humphrey was an animal man—he'd broken in horses for the Army, trained animals for circuses: he really knew what made them tick."

"He sounds really something," Steven said.

"Actually he was the one who eventually started the Guide Dog idea over here in England. News of what was going on soon got around and people started to ask why we couldn't have them, too. But we have this quarantine regulation which says dogs from other countries must spend six months in a kennel. You know—because of the danger of rabies. In six months a lot of the training would have been forgotten. The only alternative was to train the dogs here, and so they lent us Elliot Humphrey."

"Gosh, that was a gesture, wasn't it?" Steven couldn't help hoping that if the position had been reversed England would have done the same thing.

"I'm sure we would," Susan said. "Well, scientists pool their discoveries, and so do doctors. There's a phrase for it, isn't there?" She wrinkled up her forehead, thinking.

"Transcending the barriers," Steven suggested.

"Yes, that's it—transcending the barriers of class and creed and language and politics. We need our heads examined, don't we, quarreling and fighting when there must be thousands of ways like this where we could all be helping each other to live better."

"It's quite a story, anyway," Roley said, interested really only in getting himself living again, his mind unable to take in what could be done for anyone else. If it really did mean that he was going to get about on his own again—like John Morley, go where he liked, when he liked. To be independent.

"I've set lunch in the dining room," Roley's mother said, putting her head around the door. "We shall be home late and I thought we'd need something more substantial than afternoon tea. Isn't the news marvelous? I was dying to shout it down from the window to you, but I couldn't steal Roley's thunder. It was a wonderful idea of yours, Susan."

"It was more Constable Sutton's idea than mine, I'm afraid," Susan had to admit. "If he hadn't talked about them I wouldn't have dreamed of doing anything about it, Roley was so anti-dog."

"I still am," Roley assured her, "but I'm prepared to come to an arrangement with one. I'll feed it well and give it a good home. In return it had better do its stuff."

11 *Training Center*

"It smells good." Roley inhaled a deep breath, held it and let it go, slowly. The smell conjured up an old vision—open rolling fields under a wide sky, sheltering woods alive with birdsong, villages snuggling in the embracing folds of hills. "I've never smelled it so good before."

"You all say that." Relaxed behind the wheel of his open convertible, George Stretton thought again as he had thought a thousand times before how right he had been to throw over the office job in town for this job as trainer. His friends had thought him crazy: the hours were long, the pay less than he'd been get-

ting, the work exacting and hard on nerves and pa-
tience—but the reward was immeasurable. He felt this
every time he picked up a new student. This boy at
his side, helpless now and dependent on friends and
relations, would in a few weeks' time be striding out
on his own, taking an active and useful share in every-
day life again—and all because of his skill as a trainer.

"Smell and hearing," Roley said. "I feel I've never
used my nose or my ears properly before."

"The human body's a wonderful piece of mecha-
nism," George said. "One part ceases to function and
another takes over."

"All the same—one can't help remembering," Roley
said.

"That's a mug's game," George said crisply.
"There's only one way to look and that's forward."

"It's easy to talk," Roley said, aggrieved. What did
this chap know about it, sitting behind the wheel of
his car, coming and going as he felt like it?

"My father went blind," Stretton said, "and he was
an artist. He lost his job and his freedom at one blow:
and by the time dogs came on the scene he was too old
to have one. You're lucky, boy—dead lucky."

Luck! Roley could think of many names to call what
had happened to him, but not that.

"Well, how am I going to make out, do you think?"
It was the question he had been dying to ask ever since
they had set out from Barnwood three hours ago. He
wasn't sure whether he liked this trainer chap: the
hard, blunt, unsentimental attitude to the whole business of blindness was a bit of a shock after the way

everyone had played nursemaid to him. It was true he resented the way he had to accept help all the time, but he'd also taken it as his due.

"That's up to you entirely," George said easily. "I can only show you the way."

"But I thought the dogs were supposed to be trained."

"They are, highly trained," George agreed, "but they don't do the job all on their own. The two of you work as a unit. You give the orders, the dog carries them out."

"Isn't it difficult—putting your trust in a dog so completely?"

"Very difficult," Stretton said. "Nothing that's worth having comes easily. It's got to be worked for."

"John Morley said he was blind, but he came all the way from Brackley with only the dog—" Subconsciously Roley had accented the word "said" and it pinpointed the doubt and mistrust in his voice.

"John Morley's total," Stretton said. "I remember him coming to the Center. He was one of my first students. He lost his sight falling from some building scaffolding. The only difference between the two of you is that he likes dogs. You haven't much use for them, have you?"

The remark was so unexpected—and so true—that for a moment Roley couldn't think how to answer him. He had tried to be so careful not to show it.

"I—I've never had much to do with them," he said, awkwardly, "and it doesn't help that a dog was responsible for my being blinded."

"O.K., the dog lost you your sight and now your hostility against all dogs is going to lose you your chance of freedom and independence, too."

"I don't get you," Roley said guardedly, suspiciously. Someone must have said something: Susan, Steven, his parents—Doc Graham, maybe.

"No one has briefed me," Stretton assured him. "It's just my job to size up a student and how you feel about dogs stands out a mile. You asked me a moment ago how I thought you were going to make out. You're not if you don't change your attitude. I've decided to overlook it because I know about these particular dogs and I think *they'll* handle *you* in their own way, but get this straight. If you don't have a change of heart you'll be wasting my time and preventing someone else from taking advantage of the course, someone who really wants to get on with living."

The remark was a verbal slap in the face and it pulled Roley up sharply. Rotten devil, he thought: didn't he understand how it felt? He should try being blind, just for five minutes. All the same, he hadn't meant to get on the wrong side of him. He said in a moment, "I'm going to try, honestly I am."

"That's better," Stretton said. "You can either make it easier for yourself or more difficult. This is going to show what you're made of."

The country smells had gone, the swish of passing traffic and the reduced speed they were traveling at, the frequent stopping and maneuvering, could only mean they were approaching a town.

"We're a couple of miles on the other side," Stretton

told him pleasantly, "and no way of avoiding this crawl, I'm afraid."

It was a good twenty minutes before they were moving freely again and then quite soon they turned sharply and began to climb.

"The drive's a bit rough," Stretton said, "but filling in the potholes would amount to the price of several dogs—and dogs must come first."

He was a Jekyll and Hyde character, Roley decided; one moment a brute who had no vestige of feeling, the next a man completely dedicated to his job. Or was it only results he cared about and a ruthless determination to get them?

The car swept around in an arc and drew to a standstill. There was a distant clamor of barking, a kind of canine welcome, Roley supposed, and then Stretton was out of the car and opening the passenger door for Roley to get out, too.

"Welcome to the Center," he said. "Come and meet your fellow students."

Roley had the impression of a large country house—up two steps and through a wide doorway into a tiled hall.

"You won't need the stick anymore," Stretton said, taking the groping stick out of Roley's hand. "You'll soon get the geography of the house and there's a guide line down to the kennels. Ah—meet Mr. Bryant, the Controller. This is Roley Rolandson, sir."

A large hand took and gripped Roley's. The friendly warmth of it lifted Roley's spirits for the first time since he'd left home, and the voice deep and reassuring: "Glad to have you with us, Roley. I was just having a cup of tea. Come and join me. We'll see you later, Stretton." He propelled Roley across the hall and into a carpeted room warm with sunshine and sweet with the scent of flowers. "You'll be seeing quite enough of Stretton in the next few weeks."

See, seeing—didn't he realize he couldn't see? And he'd "seen" more than enough of Stretton already, Roley felt like saying, but had enough sense to keep the thought to himself.

"Mary, my dear, this is a new student. Roley, this is my wife."

Suddenly it was like home, sharing the comfortable couch with Mrs. Bryant, a cup of tea on the table by his knee, and the feeling that here were two people who really did understand. Relaxed and at ease Roley found himself talking about his own home, about what he had been going to do before—the accident, how he might still be able to take up the university course if he made the grade. He had been scathing of the future to Steven, but now he realized that hope had been there all the time, waiting for reassurance.

"Of course you'll make the grade." The Controller's voice was almost amused. "Students come and go through this Center all through the year, and year after year. I can make a pretty good guess at who's going to be in at the finish."

"You mean—some don't make it?" Roley may have had doubts himself but to hear those doubts confirmed was something else.

"In a very few cases," Mr. Bryant said. "Some have been blind too long, are not able to accept leadership and responsibility after leaning on others for so many years. Some are fundamentally incapable of controlling a dog, or of putting their trust in one—but it's rare for such people to get as far as the Center. They're pretty thoroughly sifted before they come here. Students are not usually accepted as quickly as you were, but your doctor's report was good, we had a vacancy, and I knew I could trust John Morley's judgment—and George Stretton wouldn't have brought you back with him if he'd had any doubts."

He may not have had any when they left home, Roley was thinking, but he was sure he had plenty now and wondered if he was only waiting to pass on his revised opinion to his boss. Well, he'd show him. He'd make the grade if it killed him. He'd come here for a Guide Dog and he was going to have one.

"You have a class in about half an hour," Mr. Bryant told him. "Just time to see your room and have a quick walk around the house."

"I'll give you the guided tour," Mrs. Bryant said. "It's one of my privileges as Controller's wife to show new students around." She put her hand lightly under his elbow and guided him firmly across the room.

"Thank you for the tea, sir," Roley said. "And for the talk."

"It's a lovely old Georgian mansion," Mrs. Bryant told him, walking across the hall. "We've had some alterations made inside, of course, but it's still beautiful. The staircase is the joy of my life." She placed Roley's hand on the banister rail and walked up the staircase with him but a step behind.

The rail was broad and smooth under Roley's hand, and curved gently.

"Fifteen stairs," Mrs. Bryant told him. "The corridor straight ahead is all bed-sitting rooms. You're the third room along and you're lucky, the bathroom's next door."

A narrow rail ran waist-high along the wall. Door number one—two—three. Roley found the knob and turned it.

"Divan bed on the right," Mrs. Bryant told him, "dressing table under the window, washbasin and closet on the left—and a comfortable armchair. There's a radio in all the rooms—just over the bedstead—and a push-button bell hanging beside it. We don't encourage students to use that unless they really need help because we've no extra staff. It's a good idea to pace the room," she added. "You get the shape and the feel of it right from the start."

"Ten—by—six," Roley counted out, bumping into the armchair and ending up flattened against the closet door. He felt his way back to the bed and tried it out. He had thought it might be a hospital type bed but he sank deeply into it. He lifted a hand, found the radio and turned the knob. A blare of hot jazz filled the room and he turned it off. He ran his fingers down the bell rope but didn't press the button at the base of the pear-shaped holder. "It's a comfortable room," he said. Carpet covered the floor, no loose rugs to trip over, room to walk around but nothing too far away.

"All the rooms are the same," Mrs. Bryant told him, "except for the furnishings. The men's have nice masculine draperies and covers—yours are tobacco and orange. The women's rooms are a bit frilly. You may think it doesn't matter but it does. An attractive room's good for morale. If you saw it looking messy you'd know what I mean."

"You use that word all the time, don't you?" Roley said. "Mr. Bryant did, too."

"What word?" Mrs. Bryant closed the door behind them and walked him to the end of the corridor.

"You presume we can see."

"And so you can." She took hold of his left hand and spread his fingers against her own. "You see with these and you'll find they become more and more sensitive as you get used to what is just a new way of living. A student who has the room next to yours has been blind from birth. You'll be able to compare notes." She paused, her hand on his arm. "This is the back staircase and a shortcut to the kennels—but that is George Stretton's province so we'll go back the way we came."

The dining room was to the left of the staircase, the sitting room to the right. A cheerful babble of voices flowed out to them and Roley went with her to meet it.

12   *Letter Home*

"Do you know how to use a tape recorder?" Mary Bryant's bright voice brought Roley back from the near edge of sleep. The class was finished, supper over, and too tired and depressed to stay chatting with the others, Roley had come up to his room. He hadn't undressed but just flopped back onto his bed. Now he raised himself up on an elbow and turned in the direction of her voice.

"Yes—I have one at home." It had been a present from his mother and father when he won the university grant. To begin with it had been a fascinating toy—recording music from special concerts, recording medi-

cal talks, recording himself replying to the oral questions on exam test papers. It had taken a bit of time
getting used to his own voice, quite unlike the way it
echoed in his own ears, and he'd worked at making
himself sound less of a moron.

"This is my idea and I'm proud of it," Mary Bryant
said, moving things about on the bedside table to make
room for the machine. "I expect you can use a typewriter, but with this you can ramble along as if the
people you want to talk to were here in the room. I'll
mail it for you when you're ready for it to go."

"Hey, that's great." Roley switched on the mike,
said a few words and played it back. "I was thinking
I'd telephone home, but there's so much to say."

For a long time after Mary Bryant had gone, Roley
lay with the microphone in his hand. His first reaction
had been to talk to his folks but after all it was their
voices he wanted to hear—and they would want to
hear his, in the real. He would ring them tomorrow;
by then he might have been allocated his dog and there
would be more to tell them. Right now he wanted to
get his feelings off his chest, feelings that would only
upset his parents. Funny how much easier it was to
talk to strangers, well—not strangers, but someone who
wasn't a relative. He stretched out a hand, felt around
for the recorder button, and pressed it.

"Hi, there, Steven—and Susan if she's with you. I'll
bet you didn't expect to hear from me in person. This
is an incredible place. A planet in outer space, that's
how it feels to me at the moment: new people, new
sounds, new directions to learn. It's comfortable
enough and the Controller and his wife are splendid

people, warm and friendly and helpful. The inmates
are a nice bunch, too: four women and three men
besides myself with two trainers between us. Most of
the students have been going blind gradually and are
more or less cheerfully adjusted. They've been looking
forward to this course as kids look forward to a picnic,
a picnic with a prize for everyone before they leave to
go home. Most of the talk sickens me, they're all so
grateful. Well, perhaps I'll feel grateful, too—but it's
going to take time. At the moment I can't feel obliged
to anyone for the cracks on my shins, for having to
hunt for the things I drop or mislay, for finding my
way in and out of all the wrong places, because—*boy*,
you're on your own. There's no one to wait on you
here. And George Stretton, I'm with his group—you'd
love him! Dinner was put in front of us tonight and
there we were with knives and forks and expected to
get on with it. 'Meat is at two o'clock, potatoes at four,
veg at six, and Yorkshire Pud at nine.' It took me a
minute to grasp what he was getting at—using the
clock face to position our food. I suppose it wasn't a
bad idea and I worked my way around my plate all
right, but it was odd not having it cut up for me.

"We had our first class this evening, too. And what
do you know? We're supposed to look after the dogs
ourselves. We were issued combs and brushes for
grooming them, and we're expected to feed them and
exercise them. One meal a day is all they get which
is something to be thankful for, no tidbits as rewards—
a kind word is sufficient. Whoever coined that phrase
'a dog's life' must have been here! I begin to wonder
who I'm most sorry for—me or the dog. We were

handed the harness tonight, too—to use when we take possession of the dogs. It's a kind of bridle which fixes over the dog's head and buckles around his stomach. It has a hard handle and this is our contact with the dog. You only put the harness on the dog when you want it to take you out; when the job's done you take it off and then the dog is off duty. It's a serious business, I only hope the canine wonder knows all this, too. It seems some kind of mystical message passes through the hard handle from the owner to the dog—and vice versa. Something to do with the close contact. The dog can feel the master's reaction almost before the command is given. And what do you know? We're blind but we do that as well. We give the dog the directions to get to where we want to go. I asked Stretton how and got the reply I might have expected: The same way sighted persons do—you ask.

"A nice guy has the room next to mine—Paul Bruce. He never has been able to see, which puts him in a different category. He's fabulous. He hasn't been here any longer than I have but he knows his way about as if he'd lived here all his life. When he drops something he can find it immediately: he can hear from the sound it makes just where it's fallen. He can describe things to you because he's 'brailled' them. He 'brailled' me within five minutes of our meeting and a photograp wouldn't have been more accurate. It felt a bit eerie having someone's fingers running over you but evidently it works. I suppose what you've never had you never miss. All the same, I think I'd rather be me, at least I have a mental picture of the way things are. The only other student about my own age is a girl

called Elizabeth Vaughan. She plays the piano—really
plays it and is going to teach after she's through her
Royal Academy course. Imagine that—subways and
buses and London traffic, and teaching sighted people!
I wish I could feel the way they do, full . . . of . . .
optimism . . ."

The microphone slipping out of Roley's hand woke
him up. He stretched out a sleepy arm and stopped the
tape. The peaceful quiet of his room, the sound of his
own voice, and tension relaxed for the first time since
the *thing* had happened had brought sleep flooding
over him.

He woke to the breakfast bell ringing and for a
moment lay there thinking he was back at school—but
what was going on if they were ringing the bell in the
middle of the night. He sat up—and the present came
rushing back. He slipped, very cautiously, out of bed
and felt his way to the washbasin. Maybe he'd venture
a bath before dinner but for the moment all his
thoughts were concentrated on getting down to the
dining room.

At least he wasn't the last. Paul Bruce slipped into
the chair beside him all of ten minutes later.

"I went to have a look at the dogs," he said, tucking
into the breakfast set before him.

"You're sure it wasn't the kennel maids?" someone
commented from across the table.

"I might have known I wouldn't get away with it,"
Paul said. "Well, they're O.K., too. They're handed
out to us this evening—the dogs, of course, not the
kennel maids." The corny joke shook the tables and
loosed the hesitant tongues.

"All right now," George Stretton called at last. "Class at ten o'clock, sharp."

It was just like being back at school, but with an added sense of urgency.

". . . and so you see the kind of future you're going to have depends on yourselves," George Stretton was saying, "and on what your dog thinks of you." A titter of laughter ran through the class but Stretton wasn't laughing. "Don't underestimate the animal who's about to become your guide and companion: treat her well and she'll respect you. Even if you don't treat her well she'll probably forgive you because a dog's heart is a whole lot bigger than a human being's, but she'll stop being a good guide. If you don't care, why should she? Training doesn't cease at the end of this course, it goes on each day and every day. And remember the vital link between the two of you is *your voice*. You give your commands clearly and simply—and let her know you're pleased when she carries them out correctly. Encouragement and correction and praise when she does her job well—those are the keys to success."

Stretton talked on about how the dogs had been trained to avoid obstacles by walking around them, at the same time leaving enough room for the blind person to walk around them, too; to cross the road from curb to curb moving to left or right angles with the curb, and that at the curb they will stop to receive new orders or the command to cross. And if traffic is moving on the road, even if the blind person has given the command, the dog has been taught to disobey the command until the danger has passed before moving forward again. "The dog isn't a fool," Stretton said.

"She's been taught that a moving object is a dangerous object. She isn't going to risk her own neck any more than she's going to risk yours. Now—we're going to have a practical demonstration with me as the dog. I'll take you in turn, twenty minutes each. Rolandson, I'll have you first."

With Stretton's hand on his shoulder, Roley walked from the classroom, across the hall and out into the grounds. He'd a momentary vision of Stretton on all fours, harness strapped around his middle, prancing at his side—and in his left hand the handle felt real enough.

"It's a replica of the one on the harness," Stretton told him. "Now—always the dog on your left leaving your right hand free. This will give you a 'feel' of the real thing and get you used to giving the correct commands, and there are only seven basic ones: Forward, Sit, Right and Left, Come, Stay, and Down. Now then—For-ward. Come on, repeat the command. Remember I'm the dog. I'm going to take you along this pavement until we get to the curb and then I shall wait until you tell me what to do—and I'll appreciate you talking to me so that I'll know we're good friends and doing the job together."

"For-ward!" Roley commanded feeling slightly stupid, and was instantly propelled forward at a much faster rate than he had anticipated.

"A dog moves at four miles an hour on an average," Stretton told him. "You've gotten into the habit of moving warily, but you'll soon get used to it." He stopped suddenly and Roley was pulled to a standstill beside him. "Well?" Stretton questioned.

"For-ward," Roley commanded self-consciously, and at the same time feeling for the curb with his toe. He was ready when they came to the curb on the other side.

"If you want to encourage me," Stretton said, "I answer very well to Hup-hup, the way you would say Gee-up to a horse."

They tried some left turns and some right turns, Stretton moving behind him on the turn so that Roley should not fall over him. They maneuvered around a few obstacles and then retraced their footsteps. When they got back to the house Roley felt as if he'd been on a cross-country marathan race.

"Very good," Stretton said. "You're going to do fine. Relax now and this afternoon we'll have another try. Training on the dummy handle you'll find is a great help when it comes to training with your dog. And maybe tonight we'll hand over the dogs."

After lunch there was another class and after that the "dog" race all over again. This time, prepared for what was in store, Roley did better. All very well to be sure of himself inside the grounds of the Center and with a human dog. The real test was to come, he knew that, but if the dogs really had the sense they were cracked up to have it shouldn't be too bad.

It was unusually quiet in the dining room that evening. Everyone was tired after the long, hard day— but there was more to it than that. There was a kind of undercurrent of excited anticipation, nervous·anticipation. A feeling of zero hour coming up fast. Even Paul Bruce was silent, he couldn't even manage one of his corny jokes. Elizabeth Vaughan broke the long silence.

"Suppose . . . she doesn't like me?" she said suddenly, out of her thoughts. "I mean, I like dogs but I'm not used to them. And they can tell, everyoné tells you dogs can tell if you like them or not."

"So—you like them," Stretton said consolingly. "You've nothing to worry about."

"Well, I've never actually *bitten* a dog," Paul Bruce commented, weakly.

"All right," Stretton said. "Let's put you out of your misery. If you'll all go to your rooms now and wait there I'll bring the dogs to you. This way you're all more relaxed, the dogs, too."

Roley sat on the edge of his bed. It was crazy to feel nervous just because he was meeting a dog. And it hadn't anything to do with thinking the dog might not like him: he didn't care a damn if she did or not. The dog was trained to do a job and he was being trained to use the dog. There wasn't anything more to it than that. He was prepared to feed it and groom it. To think a dog had any thoughts beyond that was sheer sickly sentimentality.

There was a scrabbling in the corridor and Stretton's voice sounding a lot warmer, a lot more sympathetic than when he spoke to the students. Roley gripped the edge of the bed as the voice and the footsteps came closer and stopped outside his door.

"Roley—this is Mick."

There was the soft thud of excited, prancing paws on the carpet and then the hurtling, squirming body hit Roley somewhere between his chest and his chin.

His recoil was automatic and instantaneous—both arms up protecting his face, his body arched away from the smothering impact. He managed to get to his feet, screaming the one word: "Down. Down. Down. Down."

There was a little whimper of surprise and disappointment and then Stretton's voice very soft, very gentle, "Down, Mick. Good girl. Good girl," and the caressing slap of his hand on the dog's flank. "We got a bit excited, didn't we? So pleased to see your new master. All she wanted was for you to touch her," he said to Roley. "Well, for God's sake, *touch* her."

The words were a command and compulsively Roley put out a hand. It bumped against a cold, wet nose, soft warm fur.

"That's better," Stretton said. "It's as strange for her as it is for you, you know. I'll leave you now to make friends."

The door closed softly behind him. It was suddenly so quiet that for a moment Roley thought the dog must have gone, too. Then the soft whimpering began again and the scrabble of claws against the woodwork of the door.

"Shut up—and Sit." Roley hurled out the words. The little sound stopped immediately, as abruptly as if the words had been well-aimed stones. In the silence Roley dropped back onto the bed, rolled over and buried his face in the pillow. "Bloody dogs," he sobbed. "Bloody, bloody dogs."

13   *Letter Home Continued*

"He's not happy there," Susan said. "It isn't going to be any good."

Roley's disembodied voice had stopped. For a moment the tape ran on and then Steven stretched out a hand and shut it off.

"That's yesterday," he said. "By now he'll be feeling quite differently about it." It wasn't really what he was thinking but he knew it was what Susan wanted to hear. This was what he had been afraid of—Roley carrying his resentment into his new life so that he couldn't see beyond it to the way it could be. And it was a shame he felt the way he did about George Stretton. The trainer probably felt he had to be tough to be helpful. Steven had used that method himself with Roley though not with the intention of bringing him to his senses, but it had—or at least it had paved the way to his accepting the idea of having a Guide Dog. Now if he wasn't careful, Roley was going to lose this wonderful opportunity to be independent again, and it wouldn't come a second time; there were too many really eager people waiting for just such a chance. The last part of Roley's recorded letter would have been funny if it hadn't been pathetic.

". . . I couldn't think what the little sound was that woke me, a grunting sound and something nudging my elbow—and then I remembered. The thing wanted to be let out—to be taken out. We'd been told all about that, 'emptying them' had been the charming way Stretton had put it, four times a day. This was the first session coming up. I'd put the harness on the armchair so I'd know where to find it, but Mick was saving me the trouble. She had it right there in her mouth. No question what I was supposed to do with it. O.K.—you've never tried putting a harness on a dog by feel. You should try it some time. It's hilarious. I got it fastened and then found I'd put it on the wrong end."

Steven couldn't help laughing. He could just see the dog, her tail coming out of the harness where her head should have been.

"I don't think it's a bit funny," Susan said, but she was laughing just the same.

"I'd like to have seen the look on Mick's face," Steven said. "Surprise? Disgust? Or maybe she was laughing, too. I think she sounds that kind of dog."

They were in Roley's bedroom, sitting on his bed, the recorder on a chair in front of them and plugged into his bedside light socket. Roley's mother, with characteristic tact, had left them alone. There was so little to tell him.

"Except that you've passed your exams," Steven reminded her. "That's plenty."

Doubts had crept in to shake her confidence at the end. She had spent so much time with Roley, and so much time thinking about him when she should have been reading—but she had passed. Now she was Sister Lambert.

"Yes, that should shake him," she agreed. "And you can tell him about your mess-mates and your first dinner in Hall." She picked up the microphone and handed it to him. "You have first innings. I'll chip in when I think you've talked about yourself long enough."

"He'd much rather hear from you and have me chip in," Steven assured her.

"Do you really think so?" The little questioning look lit her face but it was gone in an instant. "I'd like to tell him about the new pavilion they're building across at the Tennis Club, but how can I? He was one of their crack players, did you know that? It leaves you with things like the new cables the telephone people are laying in Park Place. He might be glad to know that if he's back before they finish."

The last time she and Steven had walked up Park

Place everything had been as usual. Now a deep trench yawned between the sidewalk and the road almost the whole length of the street. It was the first thought that had sprung to her mind, how a dog could be expected to negotiate a thing like that with a blind man in tow. He would have been taught to avoid lampposts and mailboxes, and trees which normally bordered the roads, but this unexpected hazard might present him with a real problem, even cause a terrible accident.

"I don't think so, really," Steven tried to reassure her. "It will be just another obstacle to get around. Well, what about building obstructions? That's the same kind of thing, isn't it?—and you never know when those are going up. It must be all part of the drill."

"It petrifies me every time I think about it," Susan said. "You must have to have such *faith* in the dog and Roley hasn't any, doesn't even like them. Honestly, I don't see how it can work."

"A month's a long time," Steven reminded her. "And don't forget, seven other people are working at it, too. Some of the atmosphere must rub off."

"I suppose you're right," Susan said, not at all convinced.

"Well, I'm not going to commiserate with him," Steven said. "I've enough teaching troubles of my own. I'll tell him about some of those." He switched on the tape and spoke into the microphone. "Hi, Roley—this is 'Judge' Lawrance reporting—"

14   *"Judge" Lawrance Reports*

" . . . I'm sorry there's no news about Charlie Phelps yet, Roley," Steven's voice came through the loud-speaker, "but maybe they're waiting until I get on the bench and can pass sentence on him myself. Then I promise you I'll let you dictate the terms."

"He's developing a very belligerent manner," Susan's voice broke in. "I'll be sorry for anyone who really crosses him."

"I didn't know it was beginning to show," Steven went on, "but if you'd like me to come down and try it out—"

"If you can spare the time," George Stretton's voice

interrupted from the doorway. "I'm taking you out with Mick this morning, remember?"

Roley's finger jabbing down on the switch and Mick's scrambling welcome across the floor drowned Steven's words, but the pleasant thought of the trainer suddenly reduced to insignificance had brought a grin to Roley's face. "Letter from home," he explained. "Sorry, I couldn't wait to play it through."

"And we do need the harness putting on, you know," Stretton's voice had an edge to it.

The harness. Where had he put the damn thing? Roley felt about in the armchair and on the bed. Stretton must be able to see it. Anyone else would have jumped to it and handed it to him.

"You could try the hook on the door," Stretton said, at last, "seeing as how it was put there for that purpose."

He'd forgotten all about the hook. Mary Bryant had pointed it out to him the night before. "If you always put it there with the leash you'll have no difficulty finding it," she'd said. "I know it doesn't come natural for boys to be neat but keeping things in the same place is a good idea and saves a lot of time and frustration."

Mick was standing by the door anyway, ready and waiting—and raring to go from the way she was squirming around.

"Stand. Stand now. Good girl." He tried to put a bit of feeling into his voice, fastening the harness around the dog's tummy. At least this time he'd gotten it on the right end. The leash as well as the harness, he was careful to remember, so that if he wanted to drop the hard handle or even if he let it go accidentally, he still had control of the dog. Well, that made sense.

"Good," Stretton said.

"Hup-hup." For the first time the little word of encouragement came naturally, but the dog at his side felt vastly different from Stretton's firm, even stride. With the staircase ahead of him he pulled desperately on the hard handle, his right hand feeling for the rail.

"Easy, easy," Stretton corrected him. "Trust her. She'll stop and sit at the head of the stairs until she gets your next order."

But if she didn't? Roley could feel his skin prickling with fearful apprehension. When he had gone through the same experience with Stretton at the other end of the hard handle there had always been the certainty that a stumble would have brought a steadying hand to his rescue. Stretton was close beside him now but not in actual contact with him—and then all at once Mick stopped and sat. Roley put out a hand and there was the rail. A little quiver of surprised incredulity shook him. He licked his lips. "Forward, Mick. Good girl." He felt for the first step, apprehensively, and found it. One, two, three—his hand gripping the rail, counting under his breath. No landing, just the gentle sweep of thirteen, fourteen, fifteen stairs.

"Good. Very good." Stretton's voice, steady and casual, reduced, suddenly, the thought that there had been any danger. The dog had brought him downstairs. It hadn't pitched him headfirst down the whole flight. It was routine—but now Mick was hesitating, twisting and pulling on the harness. Roley could *feel* the dog's uncertainty through the handle. It was as if

Mick were saying: "Hey, what is this? Do I have to go with this chap?"—turning to Stretton for orders.

"Hup-hup." Roley's voice was full of irritation, exasperation; pulling on the handle. Damn the dog, didn't she know what she was supposed to do? He imagined Stretton glowing with conceit that the dog so obviously preferred him to this new awkward master.

"Use your hands," Stretton told him. "Indicate Forward as well as directing her verbally. She's confused, expecting to get her directions from me. Give her time. Be gentle—and firm. She feels strange, that's all."

"She and I both," Roley muttered under his breath.

They crossed the hall and the sweet spring air wafting through the wide-open doors would have drawn Roley without the help of any guide. The heavy scent of hyacinths conjured up a vision of flower beds.

"Looking nice now," Stretton said as if he read Roley's thoughts. "Mrs. Bryant filled the beds under the windows with pink hyacinths last autumn and planted crocus in the lawn around the trees. I like to see them coming up naturally like that, but it drives the gardener crazy when he has to cut the grass."

Back to Dr. Jekyll, Roley registered. Who would have thought he cared a hang whether flowers grew in the garden or not? Or whether there was a garden at all? Kennels and a run for the dogs was all he would have expected Stretton to be interested in. Now, walking beside Mick, trying to keep up with her without weaving about too much, Roley suddenly had a mental picture of the Center—the old house standing on a hill, colorful flower beds edging its walls, spreading trees and flower-starred lawns running down to the entrance gate they had entered by the day he arrived. Maybe beyond that there was open country, the wild Devon moors—

The kennels were over to the right when you came out of the house, the path sloping a little and running a couple of hundred yards or so away so that probably from the main rooms they couldn't be seen at all.

"Now—obstacles," George Stretton pronounced.

The course ran at the back of the kennels, a good twenty-five-yard stretch of asphalt pavement littered with obstructions—ladders, crates, dustbins, brooms, projecting scaffolding—anything that could represent a hazard likely to be found on any street. On this course Mick and her companions had been trained, painstakingly and patiently, instilling into them the necessity of not just moving around the objects, but moving around them and at the same time leaving sufficient space for the blind master or mistress to pass safely around, too. This part of the training of the dogs never ceased to amuse and amaze Stretton—the panto-mime of coming up to the overhead obstacle and play-acting that the dogs had walked him into it and badly hurt him: the cry of pain, the banging on the over-head obstruction with his free hand while with his left knee he pushed the dog aside with a sharp "No." It seemed so unfair when the dog had already left suffi-cient room for him to pass safely around the obstacle at ground level. The wounded, puzzled look on the dog's face always stabbed at him. But miraculously, after repeating the drill over and over again, came the re-ward of seeing the dog gradually associate the "No"

and the push with the wish of her master to be given more room when it came to these overhanging obstructions. Warm and extravagant praise seemed a very small reward for a difficult lesson correctly carried out but the dogs wished for nothing more than to please. Stretton's thoughts were always the same: oh, wonderful, uncomplicated companion; faithful, obedient, patient—wanting only to serve and to please. He had trained many dogs but Mick—Mick was special. The day the puppy had come to the Training Center Stretton had picked her out from among the other bright new arrivals as the one that was that little bit brighter. The weeks of training had only confirmed his first impression. He was surprised now to realize how much it hurt to see her relegated to this youth who had not the slightest appreciation of her qualities. Words were on the tip of his tongue but he bit them back.

"You're walking down the road," Stretton told Roley, "but there are a lot of obstacles in the way. Relax, don't pull against the dog, let yourself go with her. She isn't going to crash into them and she isn't going to let you."

"Easy for you," Roley thought, furiously. "I'd just like to see you let yourself go." Every time the dog pulled him over to the left he couldn't control the flinching away from what he felt must be a brick wall coming up, or iron railing, or scaffolding. He could kind of feel the *shadow* of the obstacles as they passed them. He stumbled once, resisting the dog's swerving to one side.

"Relax, relax, relax," Stretton urged him. "Mick knows what she's doing. You must trust her."

It was not a successful lesson. They walked back to the house, Stretton disappointed, Mick puzzled and unhappy, Roley sweating, his nerves on edge and bursting with irritation.

"Take it easy, boy," Paul Bruce comforted him. "You're trying to run before you can walk. And you've got to make friends with your dog. When she knows you it'll be easier." His hand felt around for his own dog. "Good girl, Sherry. I suppose she's called that because she's the color of sherry," Paul commented, fondling the great head turned to him. "What's Mick like?"

"Oh—a Labrador. The same as yours, I suppose." Stretton had reeled off quite a spiel about her but Roley had not been specially listening. To be honest, he hadn't been all that interested.

"No two dogs are the same," Paul told him. "Sherry has a white star on her chest, her front paws are cream and her back paws dark. Oh, you're a beauty, aren't you?" He bent his head and Sherry in an ecstasy of delight thrust her cold wet nose into his face and slicked her warm velvet tongue over his cheek. Paul laughed delightedly, pushing her away from him with a gentle hand, babbling sympathetic nonsense to her.

Roley bit back the retort that sprang irresistibly to his lips. Dog lovers were a breed in themselves—but he liked Paul, admired him, and was surprised now at the stab of envy that suddenly stirred him. Envy that the dog had shown him such instantaneous and warm affection. Well, Paul deserved the best dog.

Not that Mick wasn't all right, he supposed, but the harness gave her away. He could feel the dog's uncer-

tainty through the handle, her divided attention, her hankering after Stretton. Just the sound of the trainer's voice was enough to bring Mick alertly to attention. Only the captive leash, Roley knew—and Stretton's firm rebuke—kept her from abandoning her new post altogether. Something that Elizabeth Vaughan had said came back to him now. He said to Paul, "Do you believe it's true that dogs can tell whether you like them or not? Really like them, I mean?"

Paul countered the question. "Can you tell whether someone likes you or not?"

Four or five months ago Roley would have answered without any doubts at all. Since he'd become blind he hadn't thought about it, but now Paul's question made him think about the new contacts he had made. Steven for instance. He didn't have to think twice about Steven and he knew the liking was mutual. He wasn't so sure about Susan, she was linked too closely with what had happened. He knew he liked her but her feeling for him could be—oh, continued interest in a patient, pity for his being blind. Mr. and Mrs. Bryant? Instant liking on his part and instant knowledge that they liked him. Paul Bruce, too—and that went for the other students, little as he knew them. But Stretton? He wasn't sure what the feeling was between himself and the trainer but he was pretty sure liking wasn't a part of it—on either side. "I—I guess so," he answered Paul.

"Of course you can tell," Paul declared, "so why should you imagine dogs can't? If you ask me, their instincts are much surer than ours. Ours get cluttered up with all kinds of other side issues—such as we should like people because they're relations, because we've been told to like them, because it'll hurt someone else if we don't. We make a kind of compromise. Lucky dog," he said, patting Sherry's comfortable body which was now draped across his knees. "You just like 'em or leave 'em alone. It's as simple as that, isn't it?"

Everyone seemed to be getting on better than he was, Roley thought, listening to the eager conversations in the dining room and in the lounge after the day's lessons were over. All were happy with their dogs, fearful only that they shouldn't be worthy of them! It's me, Roley thought miserably. It must be me—but I can't do anything about it. I can't. I can't.

15 *On the Town*

"Now," George Stretton said, "today we're going out into the town. A fairly quiet spot to begin with. We'll work up to heavy traffic later. We don't want to waste a lot of unnecessary time so the van will take us there and bring us back." The van was an estate car with a wired-off divider behind which the dogs rode— and they adored it, pressing eager, laughing faces up against the windows to watch the less fortunate of their breed walking.

They were into the second week of the course, nearly halfway through, and as far as Roley was concerned he was worse now than he had been at the beginning.

What little confidence he had had—and heaven knows that had been little enough—seemed to be shrinking. He did all the things to Mick that he was supposed to do—the exercising, the grooming, the feeding. The putting on of the harness was no longer the trouble it had been and he'd gotten used to navigating the staircase with Mick a step ahead of him and stopping at the top of the stairs to let him know the next move was up to him. But all that amounted to was that he'd gotten used to the house. It was going to be a different story when they got out into the streets.

"I'll take you this morning, Miss Vaughan—and you, Rolandson. This afternoon I'll take Mr. Bruce and Mrs. Marriott." If there was anyone more trouble than Roley it was Mrs. Marriott. In her middle forties, unused to dogs, her gait awkward and unsteady from relying for so long on others leading and directing and thinking for her, she was having difficulty in keeping up with her dog, difficulty in suddenly taking command—but compensating for all this was her eagerness to succeed, her determination to master her faults, and her admiration for her dog.

"You don't know how lucky you are," she had said to Roley after their first encounter with the obstacles in the grounds of the Training Center. "At your age you can do anything you put your mind to, but I'm not going to let it beat me. All my life I've been dependent on others to take me out. This is a chance to think and do for myself and it won't come again. It's *got* to work."

It had to work for him, too, Roley had told her. But

the practice of two weeks hadn't made him any more perfect.

"I'll take Miss Vaughan first," Stretton said when at last the little van pulled up. "We're going to do curb and road drill and the van is going to act as road traffic for us. We'll hope for some real traffic, but using the van makes sure we'll get some practice."

Sitting in the van waiting his own turn, Roley listened to their voices. Stretton was explaining:

"You're going to walk the full length of this road. You'll cross over six streets and then you'll turn and do the return trip. The van is going to weave in and out of the intersections but you won't be given any warning. I'll be close at hand but I'm not going to interfere with you. Now—tell Sally what you want her to do and leave the rest to her."

There was a little silence—and then Elizabeth Vaughan's warm, confident voice: "Forward, Sally. We're going to have a nice walkie . . ."

The van engine starting up drowned voice and footsteps. Sitting in it as it moved slowly forward, Roley could visualize Elizabeth and Sally walking just ahead of them, plodding along in the center of the pavement, Elizabeth's mind apprehensive and alert—as his would be when it came to his own turn—then the street crossing they must be coming up to—and then the van turned slowly to the left. Roley half expected to hear a cry of alarm from Elizabeth, or maybe feel the van swerve to avoid her, but nothing happened. The van continued on its way down the street, made a right turn and then another right turn, doubling back to the road they had left in time to once more pass in front of Elizabeth and Sally as they continued on down the road. It was as if they were playing some particularly senseless and dangerous game, Roley thought—chasing around the houses in order to arrive at the next crossing in time to frighten the daylights out of a blind girl and a dumb animal.

When the van came to a standstill at last, Elizabeth and Stretton were already there and waiting for them.

"Now, that wasn't too bad, was it?" Stretton was saying.

"It was wonderful." Elizabeth's voice had a new note of confidence in it. "On that first crossing I heard the van coming but I gave Sally the command to go Forward as you'd said and she actually took no notice of me, just stood there disobeying me until the van had passed. I know it's our own van and she probably recognized it and knew the drill, but to know when to deliberately disobey an order when you've been taught such strict obedience to it is tremendous. Good girl, Sally. Good, good girl."

"You did fine," Stretton complimented her. "If you do half as well," he said to Roley, giving him a helping hand out of the van, "I'll begin to think I'm making some progress."

It felt strange to be out in the streets instead of within the safe confines of the Center. It was like when he'd been learning to swim, Roley thought—buoyed up by water wings, tethered to the instructor's rope—and then all aids removed and there you were, on your own.

"Don't forget the hand signals," Stretton reminded

him. "It'll help you as well as the dog to get a mental picture of your direction."

Through the handle Roley could feel Mick turn to take his orders from the familiar voice, could feel the slight pull in Stretton's direction. He gave the handle an irritable little tug. "Mick—Forward."

Roley heard the van approaching before they reached the curb and automatically slowed down.

"Give Mick her head. She knows what to do," Stretton's voice prompted him.

And in a moment Mick stopped. They were at the curb. The approaching van made less sound now, but Roley could *feel* it there, somewhere just behind them, coasting, waiting for him to give Mick the command for them to step into the road. He licked his lips. "Forward, Mick."

He hadn't been able to believe that Mick really would disobey the command when he gave it—but there she was, standing her ground. At the same moment the van passed in front of them and then after a brief, cautionary pause Mick went down the curb and forward across the street, another pause for Roley to feel the curb, and they were up on the other side.

"She did that very well. Good girl. Tell her she's a good girl." Stretton's voice broke through Roley's whirling thoughts.

"Good girl. Good girl, Mick," Roley repeated mechanically. It was terrific—but she'd done it for Stretton, not for him. Well, it must be obvious to anyone. Stretton was on their heels, wasn't he? I may be blind, Roley was thinking, but I'm not a fool. The little twisting pull on the harness all the time made what

was going on as clear as if he could really see them—
the dog looking over her shoulder, checking that what
she was doing was what Stretton wanted. Roley tugged
furiously at the harness, reminding Mick who was her
real boss, and felt Stretton registering another mark
against him.

They crossed two more streets. On the third crossing
he again gave Mick the order to go Forward, and again
waited for the dog to disobey him and for the van to
pass in front of them. But this time to his surprise and
consternation Mick stepped down from the curb and
began to guide him across. Convinced that Mick had
either not seen the van, or seen it and decided it would
pull up for them anyway, Roley dug in his heels, trying
to drag the dog back to the safety of the pavement
again.

"You're all right. Go with her," Stretton's voice
stabbed at him. "There's a clear road. She knows what
she's doing. Go *on*."

Every nerve in his body quivering, Roley forced
himself to relax, to give the order again. "Forward,
Mick."

They were in midstream when Roley heard the van
coming up on their right, in front or behind them, he
couldn't tell in his panic. But on the instant Mick
stopped. Roley held his breath waiting for the thing
to hit them, but it swept by and in a moment Mick
continued forward and up the curb on the other side.

"Well, give us credit for varying the drill," Stretton
said. "You're going to meet traffic midstream. Mick
knows what she's doing. You must trust her."

After that Roley followed obediently. He didn't

relax but he tried not to give way to the tense resistance that tightened and stretched his every muscle. He
arrived back at the starting point exhausted mentally
as well as physically.

"Well, I suppose it could have been worse," Stretton commented dryly. "At least the return trip was not
too bad. Down, Mick. Down, girl. Control your dog,
Rolandson. It would help quite a lot if you could convince her that she *is* your dog. It would help, too, if
you could convince yourself of that as well."

She'll have no one but you and you know it, Roley
wanted to tell him, and on the quiet you're getting a
kick out of it. You've trained the dog, handed her
over—but she's still yours. All she's waiting for is a
look, a word from you and I'd be left high and dry.

'Well, how was it?" Paul Bruce slipped into his
place at the dining table beside Roley—late as he
usually was. "Smells like pork and apple sauce"—he
felt around his plate with his knife and fork, getting a
mental picture—"and roast potatoes. Good—my favorite grub."

Roley told him the way it had been for him. "Mick
wasn't impressed with me. Neither was Stretton," he
finished dejectedly.

"Oh, I don't suppose it's as bad as that," Paul tried
to reassure him. "You know what they all say? Halfway
through the course it feels as if your nerve is going to
go, that you're never going to make it: three quarters
of the way through it comes back and with it all your
confidence."

"Well, that's where I am right now," Roley said
grimly. "At the nerve-going stage."

"Forewarned is- forearmed," Paul said. "I took Sherry out this morning. Sorry—Sherry took me, and we had a try on our own. This afternoon I'm going to show off."

"You mean—you went into the town?" Roley stopped eating, his knife and fork poised in mid-air.

"Oh, come off it, I'm not that stupid," Paul hastened to explain. "We went up the lane at the back of the house. It's a bit rough going and there are a few trees and bushes where you don't expect them to be: reasonable hazards. Not bad practice. I wanted to break myself in before I came under the eagle eye."

It hadn't occurred to Roley to explore beyond the grounds of the Center, but with the dog, why not? It was a marvelous idea. And he'd do better, he was sure, without Stretton tailing him. Mick, too. She wouldn't be forever twisting around, making sure Stretton was still there, on the alert for the sound of his voice.

". . . and you can't miss it," Paul was saying. "Back of the house and right. It takes you to an iron gate. Sherry had been there plenty of times before, obviously."

If Sherry had been there, so must Mick have been. Roley was on the point of telling Paul that he'd try it himself, when Stretton called their attention to the rest of the day's timetable. "I'm suggesting that this evening we have a pooling of experiences," he was saying. "It's comforting to find you aren't alone in the little difficulties you encounter, and helpful to others if you can pass on any useful tips. Every student is different and every dog is different but you can all

learn something from each other. I think Miss
Vaughan and Mr. Rolandson will agree we had a very
satisfactory morning on the town and if you, Mrs.
Marriott and Mr. Bruce, will be ready as near half
past two as you can make it we'll see if you can do as
well."

"Satisfactory isn't the word I'd have used," Roley
commented to Paul. "I bet it wasn't the word Stretton
was really thinking of, either, but I suppose it's no use
putting the next customers off."

"No one can put me off," Paul assured him. "I'm
just raring to go."

Lunch over, Roley went up to his room. He
stretched out on his bed, proping the book he intended
finishing on his pillow. Books printed in Braille were
larger and heavier than the same books printed in type,
and moving one's fingers along the raised dots was
tiring—that and the sudden relaxing after the strain
of the morning must have sent him dozing off. He
woke to the sound of voices below his window and the
slam of the van door: Mrs. Marriott and Paul going off
to be put through their paces. He lay there a few
moments longer thinking about Paul, wishing he had
some of his courage and enthusiasm, envying him his
dog Sherry, almost envying him the fact that he never
had been able to see and so was suffering none of the
tortures of comparing then with now. For Paul there
was only one way to look and that was forward. The
word coming into his mind unthinkingly reminded
him of the lane and of his intention to explore it as
Paul had done.

Mick was out of her own bed in the corner whining gently, hopefully, before he had opened his mouth to call her.

"Oh, you know when there's a walk in the offing, don't you?" he said as she fauned about him, dancing in front of him as he reached up to the hook on the door for the harness. "Cupboard-love, I know. Well, this time it's you and me together. No boss-man walking behind prompting you. Just me, do you understand?"

She seemed to, leaping up at him in a frenzy of joyous agreement.

"All right, all right—you don't have to tie yourself in knots. Simmer down, now. Down." He had the leash slipped over his left wrist, his left hand gripping the hard handle. "O.K. No giving the show away, and down the back staircase so we don't run into too many inquisitive people."

The back staircase was as familiar to Roley now as the main one. He used it always in the morning taking Mick down for her first exercising of the day, almost not needing Mick's cautionary pause on the top stair. He could go down pretty quickly, too—not fumbling fearfully for each step as he had done the first week.

"To the right, Mick. Right. Good girl."

This way you had to pass under the office and then the kitchen windows. Washing the dishes from lunch was still going on, the cheerful chatter of voices rising above the clatter of pots and pans. The faded smell of onions and roast meat still hung in the air. Through the hard handle Roley felt Mick hesitate and interpreted the little quiver wrongly.

"No use looking for the boss-man on this trip. I told you, didn't I? You're stuck with me, old girl, and you'd better behave as if you liked it." He tugged at the harness, and Mick turned regretfully away from the delicious and intriguing smell.

Roley had walked around the house on several occasions but before Paul mentioned it he hadn't known anything about the path that led into a lane. Now he paused uncertainly, trying to recall Paul's directions. Back of the house and—left? Or had he said right? Roley stood for a moment considering and then decided it wasn't such a problem anyway. There wouldn't be more than one path and if they came up against a blank wall he'd soon know and they could start again.

"Left, Mick," he ordered, giving the correct hand signal, too. Stretton, he thought, would have given him a good mark for that. And he must have chosen the right direction because Mick turned obediently and led him confidently forward. The little path turned and twisted and immediately hid him from the house. Roley felt a warm rush of excitement. This was more like it, striding out on his own, free at last from kindly, well-meaning escorts. This was how it would be—And at that moment Mick came to a standstill.

Roley put out a hand and touched the ironwork of the gate. "So—we made it. Good girl. Good girl, Mick." He felt around for the handle and found that, too. But now, the gate open in front of them, Mick turned stubborn.

"Forward, Mick. *Forward.*" Roley's right hand pointed the direction impatiently, but Mick stood her ground, turning to look back over her shoulder. "Forword, Mick." Roley was pulling angrily on the harness. "Do you have to look for Stretton to O.K. every step we take?"

At the word "Stretton" Mick pulled back against the harness, whining softly.

"Oh, for heaven's sake," Roley fumed. "You're *my* dog, can't you get that into your thick skull? You're supposed to be taking me for a walk. Stretton doesn't have to come along with us every time. Soon you're going to have to do without him altogether. Now— Forward."

This time Mick moved, reluctantly but at least in the right direction. The ground underfoot was certainly rough as Paul had said—and there were plenty of obstructions from the way Mick was weaving him around them. They seemed to be climbing a little hill. It felt good though, and smelled good: a rich earthy smell, clean sweet air with the tang of the moors in it. It brought back with a rush the memory of vacations: picnics, rock-climbing, swimming. Well, no one could take this feeling of exhilaration from him—if only Mick would stop acting like a kidnapped cur. He had come to a standstill again, pulling on the harness and whimpering miserably.

"Idiot dog. Concentrate on the job, can't you? We're not going back yet, and that's final. Forward, Mick. *Forward.*" But this time Mick's mind was firmly made up. Pull on the harness as Roley might he could not budge her. "All right," Roley stormed, "have it your own way." He dropped the hard handle and slipped the leash from his wrist. "Go back to Stretton. I can manage on my own. Go on—go to him. I'll find my own way—and I'll come back when I'm ready."

Anger and frustration shook him. Dogs! Stretton may think he'd trained Mick but all he'd done was train her to be faithful to himself. She'd guide all right, but only as a duty and to please Stretton. Well, he could do without that kind of dog. He'd go back to the old stick, at least it was better than an unwilling dog. Even being on his own was better than that. He took a few cautious steps forward—but the fun had gone out of the afternoon. He'd had enough. He'd turn back now and retrace his footsteps downhill, taking his time, careful to remember the obstacles Mick had weaved him around coming up. His toe stubbed something. Not a tree, something smooth and hard, unresilient. He gave it a wider berth—and suddenly the lane was giving way underneath him. He flung his arms wide, clutching nothing as the ground came up at him with a slap of water.

He lay for a moment, dazed, while the water oozed into his shoes and seeped through his clothes. He'd fallen down some sort of hole, or a ditch half-filled with water. He moved himself cautiously. There didn't seem to be any bones broken—but where did he go from here? Where *did* he go? All sense of direction had gone. He put up a hand, groping for the side of the bank, and pushed against something soft—and live. The rough warm tongue on his cheek seemed suddenly to melt the ice-bound barrier of rankling resentment. "Oh, Mick. Mick." Roley buried his face in the soft fur of the dog's quivering body, his left arm holding

her close, close as if he would never let her go. She
hadn't deserted him. She had never intended to desert
him, had only tried to dissuade him from doing what
she knew was wrong—and dangerous. When he had
forced her, she had given way against her better judgment until to take him farther would have led to disaster: had led to disaster the moment he'd sent her
away. He had sent her away but she had refused to go.
His own stupidity had landed him in this mess, but
Mick had stayed to get him out of it.

Roley clambered up the bank and onto firm ground
again. No need to call Mick, she was there close to his
side, waiting to guide him safely back. And no resentment for the way he had treated her, only delight that
he had come to his senses and was going to use her.
He felt for the leash and the hard handle and she
pushed them into his hands. "You're worth a dozen of
me, old girl," he told her, "but I'll make it up to you,
I promise." He fastened the harness around her middle
and clipped on the leash. "Forward, Mick. Let's go
home."

Following confidently behind her slow cautious steps
they went down the lane together.

16

Dr. Jekyll

"My, whatever happened to you?" Mary Bryant's voice halted Roley before he reached the foot of the stairs.

"I did a bit of exploring," Roley told her, ruefully. "Paul Bruce told me about the lane at the back of the house. He forgot to mention the water hole."

"The water hole?" Mary Bryant followed him up the stairs. "You must get out of those clothes and into a hot bath—at once. There isn't a water hole in the lane," she said, puzzled.

"There is now," Roley assured her. "I'd be there

still if it wasn't for Mick. I *should* be there still, I've treated her so badly."

"Nonsense, I'm sure you haven't. Are you certain you *were* in the lane?"

It had never occurred to Roley that he might have made a mistake but now he was suddenly remembering how he had not been sure if Paul had said left or right from the back of the house.

"Oh no!" Mary Bryant's little shuddering cry was more graphic than any words could have been. "The lane is to the *right*."

"But the iron gate was there."

"*An* iron gate was there," Mary Bryant corrected him. "We don't use it anymore. It should have been locked but just now they're laying new drainage."

The obstacles Mick had weaved him around had been drainpipes, then, not trees and bushes as he had supposed.

"Oh, worse than that, much worse," Mary Bryant cried in horror. "At the moment there's only a narrow pathway with a ditch on *both* sides. I can't believe that Mick could have got you so far up there without you both falling in."

"She'd have got me up there and brought me back without a scratch if only I'd left it to her. She knew it was wrong from the word go but when I insisted she gave in to me until it wasn't possible to go any farther. Oh, you were terrific, Mick, really terrific." He was down on his knees, arms around her, his face buried in her soft, warm neck.

"Now you're going to spoil her," Mrs. Bryant

laughed. "A fine dog-hater you turned out to be. Get out of those wet things at once and into the bath."

Roley lay, soaking luxuriously. For the first time in months he was completely at peace with himself, with the world. More than that, under his new contentment was an undercurrent of excitement. It was going to work. It was really going to work. He was going to be able to take up his university grant after all. Mick would see him there and home again. Physiotherapy might not be so bad.

Absorbed in his thoughts he didn't hear the van until it pulled up under the wide-open bathroom window. He listened idly to the slamming of the van doors, Stretton's firm voice quieting the dogs, Mrs. Marriott apologizing for herself.

"I wasn't any good, I know I wasn't—but I'll be better tomorrow. I seem to get my feet all tied up when it comes to the turns."

"You're getting the hang of it, though." Stretton was comforting her. "You just need to concentrate on one thing at a time for the moment. You're trying too hard. You must learn to relax."

"Take a lesson from me," Paul's voice broke in. "I'm too sure of myself. I try to guide the dog, try to do her thinking for her. I'm getting the hang of the footwork, though."

"You're both doing fine," Stretton told them. "All we have to do is speed you up a bit, Mrs. Marriott, and slow you down a bit, Bruce—but it's coming."

Roley grinned to himself. He knew exactly how it had been with them. He sloshed happily in the water, reluctant to get out. Five more minutes—and then he heard Mrs. Bryant's voice.

"Am I glad to see you back. We nearly had a calamity this afternoon."

Listening to Mary Bryant retelling his adventure to Stretton, Roley lived it again, but if Mary Bryant thought of it as a calamity she'd got it wrong. It had been the most marvelous thing that could have happened, a heaven-sent miracle. If it hadn't been for the mistake he would still be hard at it bricking himself up inside his own special prison. Now he was going to be free. *Free.*

"God, I feel sorry for these dogs. Sorry for me, too."

Stretton's voice, fierce with feeling, brought Roley back to the present with a jerk.

"Mick was your favorite. Your golden girl, I know. You don't have to tell me it was a wrench for you, George, to give her up." Mrs. Bryant's voice was warm with sympathy.

"Oh, it goes on in this job," Stretton said. "Next month it'll be another—but Mick is special."

"That's why you chose to give her to Rolandson, isn't it? I've known you long enough to see through you, George."

"He needed the best," Stretton said, "just because he was so against them. I've had to be tough with him, too, and I've hated that as well. I had to make him feel *something* besides pity for himself—even if it was loathing for me. Anything to try to make him fight back."

"Well, you should be very pleased with yourself," Mrs. Bryant told him. "It's worked. Mick's going to a

good home and she's got a master who is really going
to appreciate her. Oh, by the way, if you're going up
there's a package that came for him with the midday
mail. I think it's a tape from home."

Roley scrambled out of the bath, the overheard conversation ringing in his ears like a peal of bells. Stretton—to have had thoughts like that! He was all Jekyll,
then: the Hyde part had been put on for his, Roley's,
special benefit. And oh boy, had he needed it.

Drying himself fiercely, Roley tried to get himself
into focus. What a fool he had been. Everyone trying
to help him, the only one against him—himself. This
was the second miracle of the day, he decided, slipping
into his dressing gown, that all unintentionally he had
overheard the truth.

Stretton was coming up the stairs as he came out of
the bathroom, his step as familiar as at one time his
face might have been. Roley paused, his hand on the
knob of his bedroom door, waiting for the trainer to
catch up with him.

"Package from home," Stretton greeted him. "And
what's this I've been hearing about you?"

"You've only heard the half of it," Roley told him.
"Can you spare a few minutes while I put on the sack-
cloth and ashes?"

17   *Breakthrough*

The tape was from Susan and Steven. There would be time to run it through before tea and maybe time to tell them his news, too. Roley switched it on and flung himself back on the bed to listen.

". . . and this time we have some news for you." Steven's voice had a jubilant ring in it. "It does look as if George Tate is alias Charlie Phelps—just like old P. C. Sutton said. A couple of days ago there was a robbery at Baird's, the jewelers on the corner of Market Street. A stolen car was used and later found abandoned on the edge of the heath. The car was examined for fingerprints—and what do you know? Among them were those belonging to Charlie Phelps."

Roley had been idly listening but now he jerked up on to his elbow. This was certainly his day if at last the police had got on to that thug, but Steven was saying:

"I wish I could tell you they picked him up—but he's as slippery as an eel. They did find three of the men, *and* the stolen goods. Their fingerprints had given them away—all except Charlie's. His were there all right, but the three of them swore no one else had been in on the job, swore they'd never heard of Charlie Phelps, or anyone called George Tate. Constable Sutton said it looked like another dead end—until one of their brighter boys came up with a discovery: Charlie Phelps' prints were found on the engine, under the hood. Nobody elses, just his. They were found on the dash and the steering wheel, too, but his were the only one's found on the engine. I didn't get it at first but when Constable Sutton explained, of course it was as plain as the nose on my face. Those three crooks could have been right. Charlie Phelps could have been a mechanic who'd serviced the car just before it was stolen for the job. The police have already traced the owner—and after questioning him all over again they went to the garage where he always goes for service— and that was it. A chap called George Tate had worked on the car, and guess what? He'd chucked in the job the very next day, the day the news of the robbery broke. So if he wasn't concerned in the robbery itself, he's certainly concerned about being picked up by the police. The net's closing in and he must know it. So you'd think he'd get out of the area—unless he has some unfinished business to attend to. That's what the police think and they've put a closer watch on the professor's house. They won't say how they're watching it without making Charlie-George suspicious, but Susan and I took a walk up there last night and it isn't difficult to guess. Telephone people are laying new cables up the road—I think we told you—and they've pitched their camp just below the professor's place. My bet is they have a man concealed among the engineers."

There was a confusion of sound on the tape and then Susan's voice said: "That's the legal mind working, Roley, but I think it's too obvious. Besides, all the engineers look exactly alike to me. All the same, I hope they're through laying those cables before you get back, otherwise you must keep away from that part, there are holes and huts and parked vans all over the place. . . ."

Roley, out of his new-found confidence, grinned to himself. Huts and parked vans were routine—and as for holes, he'd had personal experience of those. There wasn't anything he had to worry about anymore now he had Mick.

"Steven's just saying that Guide Dogs know all about these kinds of hazards and that the only animals likely to bump into things and fall down things are the human variety."

You're telling me, Roley laughed out loud. Steven, you never spoke a truer word.

"Mick sounds wonderful," Susan was saying, "and

we can't wait to see her—and you, of course, but you know, you've never told us what she looks like? Or why she's called Mick, which is a boy's name and she's a girl. Oh, well—I guess we'll just have to wait until we can see her for ourselves. Only two more weeks to go—less. Then we'll all be together again. Take care of yourself, Roley—"

Roley let the tape run on a few moments, making quite sure there was no more to come, and then he switched the machine off. He lay for a moment, their voices still echoing in his head: Steven's voice and Susan's, but mainly Susan's. They were together all the time: well, most of the time. On the tape they sounded so close, such good friends. Oh, come off it, he told himself, this is your day, don't go spoiling it. And what else could you expect? You—kind of—introduced them, didn't you? You couldn't have been in the picture anyway, so don't go begrudging a good man like Steven.

The banging on his bedroom door and Mick's instant and clamorous reaction jerked Roley back to the present.

"All right, hound of the Baskerville's." Paul Bruce quieted Mick, then said to Roley, "Coming down for tea?"

"Right away," Roley called back. "I'll follow you."

A place for everything and everything in its place did make sense, after all. He put on a clean shirt, climbed into his gray flannels, pulled on socks and shoes, knotted the silk cravat his mother had given him and which he'd never seen, around his neck, and tucked it into the open neck of his shirt. He slicked the comb through his hair and captured the cavorting Mick. "They really keep you at it here, Mick, don't they? Never mind, once we're on our own there'll be no one to please but ourselves."

He didn't get back to his room again until after eleven, but sleep was out of the question until he'd put Steven and Susan in the picture. All the same, he'd do his reporting from between the sheets.

Mick had already been exercised and combed. She went straight to her own basket, trod the blanket until it was just the way she liked it, and then curled up, chin on paws, blinking sleepily until Roley kicked off the second shoe and flopped onto his own bed. She was asleep before he switched on the machine—

". . . I wanted to answer your tape right away but this is real treadmill stuff and once you're with it, boy, you go. Paul Bruce came and rushed me down for tea, then there was the evening class, then supper, and after that we have a kind of get-together of experiences and let me tell you right here and now that today I was the one who took the prize."

Telling for the fourth—fifth? —sixth? time what had happened to him, excitement bubbled up afresh in Roley's voice. It wasn't possible to make anyone really understand—except of course, Stretton. He had called it a "breakthrough," and that's exactly what it had been, a break through his stone-wall resistance against being helped.

". . . and I'd got it all wrong about Stretton. He is an absolute *king*. He knew exactly the kind of treatment I needed—and the kind of dog I needed, too. I know we all think our own particular dog is the best, but Mick really is. And what about that? Giving his favorite dog to the most undeserving student who ever entered the Training Center gates. She had to go to one of us, I know, but it takes some strength of character to hand her over to the one whose only thought was to use her for what he could get out of her. And she's beautiful. A golden Labrador. No contrasting mark anywhere, pure gold—and that's what she is. Her name is really Sr. Michael—after a school in Kent. The boys and girls there had collected the whole 250 pounds to buy a Guide Dog and it was Mary Bryant's idea—of course—to give her the school's name. In any case, the female of Michael is Michele, so it amounts to the same thing. And she's got a sense of humor. I can feel it through the handle of the harness along with all the other feelings that really do come through, like when I fell into that ditch. I can see now how she must have stood there watching me and thinking: 'Of all the crazy characters! O.K., if you think you know best we'd better teach you a lesson.' I expect I'm boring you but when you meet her, you'll see I'm not exaggerating. The evening ended with Elizabeth giving us a recital—the real thing, Festival Hall stuff. She's quite a girl, I can tell you. How she can hit all those notes, the right ones, too, I can't begin to imagine. It sounded great. Well, I've ten more days to go. The testing time, Stretton calls it—working in real traffic. A few hours ago the thought would have sent cold shivers down my spine but not anymore. Where Mick guides me, I follow. I don't say I won't be holding my breath when we stop halfway across the road while cars and buses and bicycles sweep past us but I'll take good care not to show it. I want Mick to be proud of me—" Sleep had begun to weight his eyelids. His bed was warm and comfortable. From her basket he could hear Mick's gentle, regular breathing and wondered if she was perhaps dreaming of the crazy, tightrope-like walk they had taken that afternoon. Good girl, Mick. Good, good girl.

"That's all, you two," he spoke into the mike. "See you in Barnwood."

18   *Steven Walks Susan Home*

"It's like a fairy story," Susan said, stretching out a hand and turning off the switch of the tape recorder.

"And the best part of it is that Roley himself triggered off the happy ending," Steven added. Roley would have mastered the drill, he was sure, but to succeed through his own stupidity was the best way of all. "I only wish there was a success story waiting for him at this end, too."

"There's still a week to go," Susan reminded him. She tried hard to keep the disappointment out of her voice. She didn't want to think badly of the police force, and on this robbery they'd done marvelously.

On the heels of finding the abandoned car they'd found the three men *and* the stolen goods, and tracked Charlie Phelps back to the garage—but there the trail had ended again.

"The one that got away," Steven quoted. "All the same, I can smell the fire and brimstone."

Roley's mother came in then and they played the tape through again for her to hear although she'd had the story from Roley himself over the telephone the night before.

"You must come to the Welcome Home party," she said as she walked to the gate with them. "Roley said there was to be no chocolate or tidbits for Mick—just a lot of affection and a comfortable bed in his own room. His father and I are going out tomorrow to buy the best there is."

"I'm so happy," Susan said as she and Steven walked down the road. "I was so afraid he was going to come back with that chip still on his shoulder. Nothing can give him back his sight, but this is the next best thing. He's free to go where he likes when he likes—and with a friend and companion who'll never let him down."

"It's going on all the time, too, this Guide Dogs for the blind business. That's what's so staggering," Steven said. "And if I hadn't become involved with Roley I might never have known anything about it."

"What about me?" Susan said. "I'm in nursing and I didn't know about them. The only excuse I've got is that Roley's the first blind patient I've had any dealings with and I suppose in the hospital the main concern is to get a patient on his feet again."

"They sound like a nice bunch he's with," Steven

said. "I like the sound of Paul Bruce—but it isn't so bad for him when he hasn't known anything different. I mean, he hasn't had anything to unlearn, having a dog is just a step forward for him."

"And Elizabeth Vaughan." Only that one name had stood out as far as Susan was concerned. She tried to remember everything Roley had said about her: ". . . about my own age . . . plays the piano . . . going to teach after she's through her Royal Academy course." And later, speaking about her, he had dropped her surname. She'd become plain "Elizabeth": ". . . Elizabeth giving us a recital . . . the real thing. My kind of music."

Out of her own thoughts Susan added, "And they've got such a lot in common."

Steven said, "Yes—I thought so, too," and added: "You don't mind, do you?"

"No. No, of course not." She put a brightness into her voice that she didn't feel. "In a way it's—well, romantic. They've both shared the same experience, they're both going to make something of themselves. Roley will, I know."

They'd come to the Crescent where Heath View divided, one half of it becoming Oakwood Drive where Steven's home was and the other half becoming Park Place and a shortcut past the tennis courts to Park Road and the hospital at the far end.

"You don't have to walk me back," Susan told him.

"I'd like to, though," Steven said.

"You have to be up early and you should be getting a good night's rest."

"Yes, Nurse," Steven said, taking not the slightest

notice, urging her forward along Park Place. "Besides, this is where the professor lives. I don't want you coming up against any lurking characters."

"You can't mean the old night watchman." Susan laughed as they came abreast of the post-office excavations. A muffled figure sat by a glowing brazier, lazy smoke twisting in a rough halo above his bent head.

"Good evening," Steven called as they passed.

"Evening," the old man answered him, lifting a hand to touch his hat.

"You can't really think he's a policeman in disguise," Susan protested. They were coming up to the professor's house now, or at least to the high wall that surrounded and hid it from sight.

"I wouldn't like to swear he wasn't," Steven said. "Though with that barricade of bricks I don't see how anyone could break in."

"Which, of course, is why Charlie Phelps used the mail delivery service."

"Well, that's what a police guard will screen," Steven said, "anyone trying to gain access, however normal the conditions."

"You're talking like a lawyer again," Susan laughed. They crossed the road to walk along by the tennis courts. It was a clear, starry evening, with a moon not up yet but throwing its light before it. The court markings glowed palely, and beyond, the building that was to be the new pavilion sat squatly behind its erection of scaffolding like some ghostly ruin.

"Roley must feel sick about his tennis," Susan said. "It was what he liked more than anything else."

"He might have grown out of it," Steven told her. "I mean, crazes don't last."

"I think it was more than a craze," Susan said. "He liked the exercise, too."

"Well, he's going to get plenty of that with Mick," Steven reminded her.

They parted, reluctantly on Steven's part, outside the hospital gates. "It's pretty grim, isn't it—living on the job?"

"No more than your university will be when you're living in," she told him. "That's what you're going to do next term, remember."

He had a real home to go back to though, weekends and vacations, but he kept that observation to himself.

"Am I going to see you tomorrow?" he asked her.

She shook her head. "I'm on nights for a while. My next time off is the Welcome Home party day. Wouldn't you know I'd have that fixed?"

"I'll see you at the station, then, Welcome Home party day. Roley's train gets in on the dot of three."

"I'll be there a little before that," Susan said, "in case it's ahead of time."

"O.K.—see you then."

He waited while she went quickly up the short drive to the hospital entrance. She looked back and waved and then the great building swallowed her up.

19 *Charlie Phelps Asks For Police Protection*

Constable Sutton was doing the last lap of his beat. It was the one that at the moment he was giving the most care to: Park Place. It had made it more complicated since the telephone people moved in. They were all over the place, testing the instruments up and down the road, sitting doubled over in their own special holes in the ground, talking over private wires in some incomprehensible language to their cohorts in other parts of the road. The chief engineer was helpful, though, if a little irritated.

"Look, chum, the answer's still the same. I know all my men. I'd spot a stranger before you could say Copper. Well, they're as good as in uniform, aren't they?"

In uniform but not a particularly exclusive one, Constable Sutton thought, looking at their tight jeans and black leather jackets: almost any young rowdy looked the same—but he kept his observation to himself. "How long's this bunch been with you? Any newcomers?"

"I tell you I know 'em all, been with me every last one of them for the last six months. Does that answer your question?"

Constable Sutton was unconvinced. It was one of the things you learned very early in your training as a policeman—to trust no one but yourself and your own two eyes about anything. "You don't know crooks like I do," he said. "Oh well, at least if you do see anyone acting suspiciously you can get a telephone message to the station pretty quickly."

"We should be drawing extra pay," the chief engineer told him. "Haven't you thought of planting one of your own men?"

"Sure, got one up the road, but it seems like sense to make use of you people, too."

He walked on, coming in a few moments to the professor's boundary wall. It was high enough to discourage anyone who had thoughts of scaling it, and the broken glass cemented into the top wasn't exactly inviting—but not a serious deterrent to someone who meant business: a jacket thrown over the jagged battlement, a boost from a pal and you were there. He

stopped in front of the black oak, iron-studded door
and tried the handle. It was locked tightly and there
was no tumultuous answering attack from the other
side: the professor had gotten rid of his dog immediately after Roley's accident. Foolish, the constable
thought, to leave himself alone in that big house and
unprotected, but understandable after what had happened.

He crossed over the road to where the hedge of the
grounds of the Barnwood Tennis Club barely topped
the low wooden fencing. Games seen from the road
brought in quite a few new members and now the
pavilion rising impressively behind its scaffolding gave
promise of much improved facilities. One of the
groundsmen was working in the shrubbery, clearing
away last year's dead wood and rotting leaves, his back
bent to the job. Constable Sutton called: "How's it
going, John? Seen any good crooks lately?"

The man raised his head and stretched himself ex-
aggeratedly. "Seems a mug's game to me," he said.
"Who's going to plan the same trick twice? I think
Charlie Phelps has more sense than to show his face
around here again."

"He doesn't have more sense than to still hang
around the area," Constable Sutton reminded him.
"And he isn't going to use the same method. A smart
boy like that will have a fresh idea up his sleeve. We've
just got to be that bit smarter, that's all. And be prepared to wait."

"You're not doing gardening duty," the man said.
"Did I ever tell you that I chose to live in an apartment
to avoid this. You just can't win."

Constable Sutton laughed. "The exercise will do you good," he said. "And the fresh air." He moved off.

"Thanks a lot," the man called after him, and went back to his desultory sweeping of the dead leaves.

One of the chief engineer's boys was coming down the road ahead of the constable. He carried a length of wire and what looked like a testing meter in one hand, and a bunch of tools in the other. The chief engineer was quite right, the whole gang were as alike as a row of ninepins—except that this one looked as if he'd had a battering at some time: an ugly scar ran down one side of his face half closing an eyelid. The youth stopped as he came alongside the constable and spat out the dead stub end of a cigarette that was sticking to his lower lip.

"Could I ask you to come with me to the big house, Constable? It's the one you're watching, isn't it? I've got a test to carry out there and I don't particularly want to go in without a police escort."

"I don't blame you," Constable Sutton said and turned to walk back the way he had come, falling into step beside the youth. "I'll see you into the house, anyway, and put the professor's mind at rest. He's a tough old boy to stick it there on his own."

"Yeah—wouldn't get me to stay there if anyone'd sent me threatening letters and phoned me in the middle of the night. He's asking for it, all right."

"Well, that's what we're here for," Constable Sutton said, "to protect him and put a stop to jokes like that."

They had come up to the door now and Constable Sutton put up a hand and rang the bell. It was quite a moment before anything happened and then a distant door was heard opening and shuffling footsteps crossing the yard. "Who is it?" a thin voice asked.

"It's all right, Professor. It's Constable Sutton."

There was a fumbling on the other side of the door and then it was opened cautiously—as far as the safety-chain on the other side would allow it. A bespectacled face topped by a halo of thin, wispy gray hair peered at them through the narrow gap.

"It's only one of the telephone engineers to test your phone." Constable Sutton set him at ease.

"What, again?" the professor complained, slipping back the chain. "Don't take any chances, that's what you said," he reminded the constable.

"Be the last time we trouble you, Grandpa," the youth said, pushing past him and making his own way across the yard and into the house.

"No respect nowadays," the professor said, shaking his head.

"Yes, that's the way it goes," Constable Sutton agreed. "Nothing else to report while I'm here? No more letters? No more telephone calls?"

"No," the old gentleman told him. "I think I've nothing to worry about while there are so many people in the road. People who are up to no good like the place to themselves."

"Can't be too careful, though," the constable said. When you'd been in the job as long as he had you didn't take anything for granted. "Well, I'll be getting along—and I still say don't take any chances."

He walked on up the road, but slowly. Something was knocking on his mind softly like a finger in a velvet glove, something the youth had said. Something that was sticking out of the mental pigeonhole into which it should have slipped unnoticed. "You wouldn't get me to stay there if anyone'd sent me threatening letters . . . or phoned me in the middle of the night." That was it. What did that youth know about threatening letters and the telephone calls? Only the professor and the police, and Roley's small circle of relations and friends, had been told about them: in which case—Constable Sutton wheeled around and began to run and with each stride a fresh thought exploded in his mind. Wasn't the telephone repair gang the perfect cover for someone who wanted to get into a house? And that scar—The conversation they'd had at the boy's home was beating now like a tattoo—"Supposing he doesn't look like his description anymore," Roland-son had said. "Supposing he isn't disguised—but disfigured?" Retaliation—that's what the scar had prompted. The constable had reached the gate now and was through it and across the yard while the rest of the puzzle was slipping into place, bit by bit, his mind taking over now to guess at what he couldn't know: the testing meter and the wire were a blind, but the tools were for serious use.

The youth was just putting the telephone receiver back on its cradle, mission completed. The professor hovered in the background waiting to show him off the premises and lock up again behind him. The flying blow that the constable caught the youth in the stomach with sent him to the floor like a felled tree. The professor took a step forward and then drew back in

amazed terror as the constable seized the telephone
instrument in both hands, tugged it away from its
mooring cable on the wainscot, ran to the door and
flung it with all his strength out into the courtyard.

20 *A Man with a Dog*

The explosion stopped Susan and Steven in their tracks as they came down the road on their way to the station to meet Roley. They had met accidentally in the Crescent—but not without design on Steven's part. Now they took one look at each other and without a word began to run.

From his bivouac in Park Place the chief telephone engineer began to run, too, his squad of men at his heels. The thin drifting smoke and the choking smell of cordite met them before they reached the courtyard, and then the professor's voice shocked and shaken:

"I can't believe it. Coming in and fixing it—right under my nose."

"What about me?" Constable Sutton was saying. "Is my face going to be red when I tell them at the station. Real nerve getting me to bring him in. That was bright on the spur of the moment, if you like."

"If anyone's face ought to be red, mine should," the chief engineer told him, going over to where Charlie Phelps was beginning painfully to stir. "Leather jacket, jeans—the lot—but that face doesn't belong to anyone I know."

The groundsman from the Tennis Club had arrived now. "I saw him coming down the road," he said to Constable Sutton. "I was just going to apprehend him and then I saw you'd taken over. Too many cooks," he muttered under his breath.

"Is it really Charlie Phelps?" Susan had pushed forward to see for herself what he looked like. He had the fresh complexion all right, but his hair—what there was of it—was dark and crew-cut. And Constable Sutton had said he was good-looking.

"What happened?" Steven had picked his way over to the remains of a telephone in the yard and now he was staring at the torn-away cord trailing from the wainscot.

"Posed as one of the telephone engineers," Constable Sutton told him. "Planted a stick of gelignite and a fuse in the box. It only needed someone to lift the receiver—"

Charlie Phelps was on his feet shouting and pointing at the professor accusingly. "He's the one to go after. All I wanted was to smash up his face like he smashed mine. He lost me my girl. I've trailed him ever since. Got myself a job here until I thought up how I'd do it and then what do you know? His typewriter came into the shop for repair."

"Your girl had a lucky break," Constable Sutton told him. "The boy you blinded wasn't so lucky. You're going to have that on your conscience for the rest of your life—if you have a conscience. Just be thankful you aren't facing a charge of manslaughter." He turned to the chief engineer. "If we could use your telephone now," he said, "I'll have a car sent up."

"You'd better stay with the joker," the chief engineer said. "I'll put the call through for you. What will he get?" he asked the constable as they walked to the door together.

"Causing grievous bodily harm? Depends on the magistrate," the constable said. "They're getting tough with these cases—and none too soon." He turned back into the hall.

"We'd better be pushing, too," Steven said, "if we want to be at the station before Roley's train gets in."

They began to follow the chief engineer down the road but suddenly Steven was standing his ground, staring past him and past the Post Office upheaval to a man coming up the road. A man with a dog. A young man, striding out, shoulders erect, head back, his hand gripping the hard handle of a white harness fastened to the dog: a golden Labrador walking a step ahead of her master.

"It's Roley!" Susan grasped Steven by the arm, not able to get any more words out for the lump that suddenly filled her throat.

Man and dog were coming up to where the telephone work filled the pavement and spilled out into the road, and to the hole fenced around by only a flimsy tripod of wood. Susan held her breath and then involuntarily moved forward to run to his aid, but Steven held her back. Without any hesitation the dog moved out to the curb, paused a moment, and then walked her master into the road, around the obstruction, and back onto the safety of the pavement again.

"Roley—" And this time no restraining hand could have held Susan.

"I caught the early train," Roley explained after the first excited greetings were over. "I had a feeling there might be a reception committee at the station."

"And we *told* you to avoid this road." Susan couldn't take her eyes off him. This was such a different Roley from the one who had left them, reluctantly, to accept the aid of a dog. He looked so fit—and well—and full of confidence.

"That's why I took it." Roley laughed. "Well, Mick was dying to show off. I couldn't let her miss a chance like this." He pulled the dog closer into the circle. "Meet the best friend a man ever had."

"Oh, she's gorgeous." Susan was down on her knees, her arms encircling Mick's frenziedly quivering body. "You're gorgeous, aren't you? Beautiful girl. Oh, Roley, she's lovely." She straightened up, restraining the delighted dog. The news they had to tell Roley couldn't wait a moment longer. "You just missed all the excitement. What do you think? Charlie Phelps was caught not a quarter of an hour ago—and by Constable Sutton."

Somehow for himself revenge didn't seem important now, but it was good that Phelps wasn't at large anymore. "Oh, no," he said. "That's wonderful."

"There's so much to tell you," Susan said, squeezing his arm.

This was it coming up, Roley thought. Well, he'd got his freedom, his independence: what more could he expect? "Can I guess?" he asked her, putting as much bright interest into his voice as he could muster.

"Guess? Guess what?" Susan asked him, puzzled.

Suddenly Roley was embarrassed. "Why . . . you and Steven. I thought . . ."

It took a moment for Susan to understand what he did think and then it was she who was embarrassed. Steven said, quickly bridging the awkward moment, "I don't mind telling you, Roley, I was working on it."

Susan looked at him in amazement. "Steven—I'd no idea."

"I know you hadn't," Steven said. "I got the message all right, though, without even having to ask. I know when the competition's too strong."

"Competition?" Roley tried to keep his voice light, make it sound as if none of this really concerned him at all. "Of course you'd got competition, Steven. What did you expect with a girl like Susan? Who is it, Susan? There shouldn't be any secrets among friends."

"Well, as a matter of fact, Steven's right," she said, tucking a hand under Roley's free right arm. "Who do you think it is? I'll give you just one guess."

The Author

Young readers probably know DOROTHY CLEWES best for her marvelous mysteries and that remarkable family who solves them, the Hadleys. Mrs. Clewes is a veteran traveler and she puts her experiences to good use. For each of her mysteries is set in an interesting locale she has visited.

With *Guide Dog*, Dorothy Clewes' writing takes on a new dimension. For she has turned her attention to a very real human problem, blindness. And with a sure understanding of young people, she has presented a moving picture of an active and vigorous young man thrust into a world of darkness. To do the actual research for her story, Mrs. Clewes visited guide dog training centers both in England and the United States. It is interesting to note that while German shepherds are used in this country, England uses Labrador retrievers exclusively.

Dorothy Clewes lives in Kent, England, but she is a frequent visitor to the United States.

The Artist

PETER BURCHARD has illustrated more than fifty books for both adults and children.

During World War II he served in the U. S. Army Signal Corps as a radio operator on a troop transport in the North Atlantic. His first published drawings appeared in *Yank* magazine.

He was graduated from the Philadelphia Museum School of Art in 1947.

Mr. Burchard is also the author of two very successful Civil War stories for young people—*Jed, The Story of a Yankee Soldier and a Southern Boy* and *North by Night*.